SETUP ON

FRONT STREET

SETUP ON FRONT STREET

by
Mike Dennis

Published by Mike Dennis

Copyright 2011 by Mike Dennis

Cover designed by Jeroen ten Berge

Ebook creation by Dellaster Design

2/12

ACKNOWLEDGEMENTS

Years ago, when I was playing music for a living and without any aspirations to writing whatsoever, it was Marda Burton, New Orleans writer, who convinced me I could become a novelist. At her urging, I sat down and began the terrifying task of putting a made-up story on paper. *Setup On Front Street* isn't my first novel, nor my last, but Marda is just as responsible for this one as she has been for every one that I will ever write.

Thanks to Joe Konrath, Amanda Hocking, Barry Eisler, and so many other successful independent authors who have finally opened my eyes to the realities of publishing. Without their trailblazing efforts, I'd still be sending out query letters to uninterested agents who often don't even bother to respond with a rejection note.

Thanks to Wes Hunter of Truman-White Chevron in Key West for the info on the big Buick Electra 225. I needed a car like that for a situation in this book and Wes was kind enough to explain it all to me.

And speaking of Key West, I want to thank all my friends here on this beautiful island for their support and encouragement, and a big thanks to Key West itself for being a great noir city. You won't find any of the clichéd Margaritaville stereotypes in these pages.

For Vince...

I wish you had lived to see this.

You have to be quick. And able.
Or you'll be dead.

Mickey Spillane, 1950

SETUP ON FRONT STREET

ONE

March, 1991

I got back to Key West on the day Aldo Ray died.

This kid sitting next to me on the bus had one of those old transistor radios, and the news crackled out of it somewhere south of Miami. The big C got him, it said.

Ray was one of my favorite Hollywood tough guys. Like myself, he was powerfully built, with a harsh, scratchy voice, cutting a bearish figure on the big screen. But he had a well-hidden, squishy-soft center, which usually meant big trouble for the characters he portrayed.

As the Greyhound made its way down the Keys that morning, I gazed out at the hot, lazy island hamlets, thinking about Ray and about what I had to

1

do.

And there could be no room for squishiness.

***

We lumbered into the downtown Key West terminal. I stepped off the air-cooled bus into the steamy embrace of the thick humidity I remembered from long ago. I started sweating right away. As I took a full stretch, my bones creaked and cracked, and I frowned.

Three days on a bus gives you the creaky bones.

Three years in the joint gives you the frown.

The passengers stood around: an odds-and-ends collection of smelly backpackers, Jap tourists here on the cheap, plus a couple of scowling Miami jigs—low-grade street types draped in gold, probably down here to make a dope drop.

As soon as the driver pulled the bags out of the belly of the bus, I snatched mine and headed across the small parking lot for a little rooming house nearby on Angela Street. It wasn't even a two-minute walk, but by the time I got there, splotches of sweat had stained the front and back of my guayabera.

Welcome home, pal.

Inside, I signed the register, then paid the deposit. I

paused for just a moment, looking at my signature. "Don Roy Doyle," it read. That was the first time in a long time that I'd written my name for anything other than prison shit.

Before my frown dissolved at this liberating thought, I remembered what got me sent up in the first place.

The clerk pushed me the key. I headed upstairs with more than a little snap in my step. Slipping the key into the lock, I gave it a turn. Then I stepped back just a shade.

I cracked the door a couple of inches, but I didn't push it all the way in. Instead, I closed it again, then reopened it. Opening my own door. With my own key. How long had it been?

The room was boiling. I flipped the AC on high, then peeled off my clothes. With nobody around.

By normal standards, I'm sure it was just an average-sized room, but compared to my Nevada cell, it seemed gigantic. It was a lot more space and a far better view than I'd been used to, and it was all mine.

Smiling, I turned the light on and off a few times, watching the bulb react to my switch-clicking. Then I moved to the center of the room where I stretched my arms out as far as they would go. I turned a couple of complete three-sixties without touching anything.

With those luxuries under my belt, I checked out the rack. It was huge, compared to the little slab I'd slept on for years. I hadn't had my feet up in three days and sweet sleep was calling me.

I didn't even pull back the covers.

***

I came to at twilight. The humming AC cooled the room to perfection. I felt rested for the first time since I left Nevada. I took a long, warm shower in wonderful solitude, without worrying about anyone trying to fuck with me.

Afterward, I pulled a fresh guayabera and a clean pair of cotton pants out of my bag. I could wear what I wanted now, so I took my own sweet time getting dressed.

With my brushed-back hair still wet, I headed down the stairs, out into the warm night. Man, I felt great.

And now, it was showtime.

SETUP ON FRONT STREET

TWO

First stop, Sullivan's.

Right in the heart of Duval Street, Key West's main drag. It was still happening, still the Keys' hottest Irish pub, packed with tourists and fancy-assed locals, slamming back the whiskey and cold brew as fast as it could be poured.

Not my kind of place, but so what.

People crammed the tables along the wall opposite the bar, wanting to feel the music coming from the high-energy piano player in the window. No Irish folk songs here, only hard-driving rock & roll. Dancers filled the aisle down the center.

The AC blew full bore, but it was no use in this crowd. Hairdos, which earlier in the evening had poofed up perfectly in the mirror at home, now hung limp over sweaty foreheads.

Almost buried in the racket, the continuous ringing of the cash register bled through. Nothing had changed in three years.

I shoved my way to the rear of the club where I spotted him in his usual seat in the far corner. There were a couple of others at the table with him, including a cooing brunette, not his wife, running long manicured fingers through his hair. She had his total attention, so he didn't see me until I was right up on him.

"Hello, Sully," I said, disregarding the others.

It startled him.

I sat down without being invited while I waited for him to say something. Finally, he gathered himself.

"Don Roy! Well, son of a gun! When'd you get back?" He stuck out his hand.

I shook it, raising my voice to be heard above the music. "Fresh out. Just got in today."

My eyes scanned the room, taking in the frenzied activity.

"Looks like things have gone pretty well since I've been gone. Real well." His nod said they did.

Sully didn't look like he'd changed any at all. He hadn't added any weight to his slender frame, while his well-preserved boyish face showed dollar-green eyes, still cold and indifferent.

—
6

SETUP ON FRONT STREET

We looked at each other for a second. Then I said, "Let's go upstairs for a minute." I picked up a napkin from the table and wiped sweat off my neck and forehead.

The piano player kicked off a Jerry Lee Lewis tune as Sully excused himself. We got up from the table, heading for the back steps to the office.

The office.

It was more like Sully's tribute to himself. Quiet lighting and tasteful furniture were upstaged by dozens of photos on the walls. Tacky framed pictures of Sully with his arm around various VIPs reminded visitors of his respectability. Most were taken during his ten years in Key West, but a few offered glimmers into his New Orleans past.

There he is with rogue governor Edwin Edwards.

Here's one with aging mobster Carlos Marcello.

Over here, he's getting the bear hug from Al Hirt, while French Quarter emperor AJ Frechette looks on.

I had to admit, not bad for a tough New Orleans Irish Channel kid named Frankie Sullivan, who started from zero.

Now, according to this fancy-looking Chamber of Commerce certificate decorating the wall above his desk, his grifter days are behind him. The Chamber conveniently forgot to include in that certificate that he

—

7

came here a few years ago on the lam, and now he's Mister Francis X Sullivan, solid citizen and dispenser of good times to those who count here on this island at the end of the road.

He moved around behind the desk and sat in the big chair. Even though he was a little guy, he seemed to fill it up. I took the seat in front. The desk was big, too big, made of dark wood. *Great Balls of Fire* was only faintly audible from downstairs.

"So, you look good," he said uneasily. "You've slimmed down a little."

"Prison'll do that."

"A little gray around the temples, too, huh?" He fingered his temples, saying, "Yeah, we're getting to that age, you know. I'll be forty-six next time. You and me, we're about the same age, right?"

His hair was still brown all over, with glints of red reflecting in the office light.

"I just turned forty." I didn't like saying that.

He reached into a desk drawer for a fresh pack of cigarettes. I could tell he was trying not to notice that I never took my eyes off him, off his every movement. He slowly stripped off the cellophane top, then shook a few partway out of the package and held it out toward me.

"No, thanks," I said. "I quit right after I got locked

—

up."

"You quit? Hey, way to go. I wish I could do it. Was it hard?"

"Cigarettes are like money in there. It's like smoking dollar bills."

"Really?"

"No point to it. When I looked at it like that, it made quitting a lot easier."

He nodded and stuck one between his lips.

"Listen, boyo, I was real sorry to hear about your mom. She was a great lady."

I looked away. "At least she didn't suffer much."

"Thank God. We should all be so lucky. Too bad it happened after you went away. She's in heaven right now, I know."

He flicked his gold lighter. The flame licked the tip of the cigarette, then he pulled in the first drag, a deep inhale. He let out the smoke in a thin, gray curl toward the ceiling. For just a split second, I thought about having one, it looked so good.

I wanted to move on to something else. He picked up on it.

"Man, we just had the biggest St Paddy's day ever. You shoulda been here. The town was mobbed with tourists and the Irish ambassador himself was here from Washington. Miami TV was here to cover it. BK

—
9

was here—oh, did you know, he's the mayor now after taking over from his daddy? Like, who didn't see that coming, right? Anyway, all the local bigshots showed up."

He leaned back, drawing again on his cigarette. He blew a perfect smoke ring to celebrate this big event. He looked like he was finished with this story, but then he added, "We took in thirteen grand!"

That wasn't what I wanted to talk about, either.

I saw the Bushmill's bottle on the shelf to my left, along with several rocks glasses lined up around it. I reached for it, then poured a shot into one of the glasses.

I gently sipped the magic fluid, pushing back the temptation to chug it. My first taste of Irish whiskey in three years. It was the good stuff: single malt, ten years old. It went down slow and warm.

For just a moment, I remembered back to when I was a teenager, watching my grandfather drinking this stuff from a private stash. He and my grandmother didn't have much money, but he'd sometimes manage to save up enough to buy a bottle of the single malt, then he'd squirrel it away so she wouldn't find it. He used to tell me about one of our ancestors—I forget which one—who was a bigshot at the Bushmill's distillery over in Ireland way back when.

SETUP ON FRONT STREET

I almost smiled.

"Thirteen grand's pretty strong, Sully."

"Damn right it is. And it's gonna get stronger. I'm thinkin' of opening another Sullivan's up in South Beach. And get this. I got an angle to move into Cuba when they open things up down there. Should be pretty soon now."

"Cuba?"

"Oh, man. It's gonna be great. Castro'll be history by the end of the year, you know, now that the Soviet Union is no more. The Russians are gone, so he's on his way out. And when he goes, things are gonna explode here."

"You think so?"

"Well, you know they don't have shit down there right now. There's all kinds of shortages all over the damn place. And the infrastructure? Forget it. They won't be able to accommodate a lot of tourists for quite a while because they need everything."

"Everything?"

Damn right. They need telephones, gasoline, good hotels, fucking toilet paper, the whole ball of wax. Paved roads, every goddamn thing."

"Really."

"No shit. It's gonna be years before they're really ready for the huge number of Americans who want to go there. And until then, a lot of people are gonna stay here and in Miami, in real hotels, and just take short day trips to Cuba. Man, this is where it's at right now."

"You said you're working an angle to move down there?"

"I can't tell you about it now, cause it's still in the planning stages, but the deal kind of involves BK."

"What's BK got to do with it?"

"Well...I can't really say anything just yet, but he's behind it."

"Sounds like you've got big plans, Sully."

I sipped slowly at the Irish whiskey.

"Expansion. That's what it's all about. Hey, man, you got to move up or move out. This is the nineties, you know?"

This was only 1991, but I was already tired of hearing people say, "This is the nineties." The way they said it, I don't know, it was like it excused any type of idiotic behavior or off-the-wall attitude. *Hey, I know I'm an asshole, but so what! This is the nineties!*

I hated it.

They'd even picked up on it in the joint. It looked like I was in for another nine years of it, but I swear, if I heard even one more person say it...

"So, uh, what're you gonna do now? I mean, now that you're back."

SETUP ON FRONT STREET

I took another sip without taking my eyes off him.
"You know what I want."

He paused and looked at his cigarette, but he didn't
flinch.

"Sure, I know what you want. You want about two
hundred thousand that you think you've got coming to
you from our Vegas swindle."

"*Think* I've got coming to me? *Think* I've got
coming? I don't think anything. I *know* we got nearly a
half a million from it. Take out our planning costs,
including the fake diamonds, and that leaves about two
hundred K apiece."

He leaned forward in his chair and looked straight
at me. Then he said in a voice as cold as his eyes, "Yes,
it does. But let me tell you something, boyo. There *is* no
money."

The Bushmill's suddenly ignited in my stomach.

"What do you mean, there is no money?

"I mean, it's not here. I invested it. My share, too!"

"Invested it? What the fuck are you talking about?"

"I'm telling you straight. I washed it through the
club and then, you know, I gave it to a legit guy, an
investment counselor up in Miami, and he put it to
work for us in straight-up investments. Like these
groups that invest in apartment complexes and office
buildings and shit."

"Office buildings? You're telling me my money wound up in some fucking office building somewhere?"

"It went into a tax-sheltered corporation with a bunch of other people's money. It's like an investment. Look at it as planning for your retirement. I can't have that kind of cash just lying around here. This way, you actually own part of these properties. I think he said there's one up in North Carolina, and another one somewhere near Houston...or was it Dallas?"

He gazed off toward the ceiling while he dragged another deep one on his cigarette.

Now it was my turn to lean forward. I did, all the way across the desk. I opened my mouth, then pulled back my cheek, showing an empty space where quite a few back teeth used to be.

"Look at this, motherfucker! Are you telling me that I fought off niggers and Mexicans for three years so I could come back and hear this bullshit?"

"Hey, I know it was tough for you. But don't forget, I took a big chance. When we got ratted out, you may have taken the fall, but I snuffed the rat. A capital offense, in case you've forgotten."

I swept my arm hard across his desk. His fancy pen holder, his desk calendar, his telephone, the picture of his wife, it all went flying across the room.

SETUP ON FRONT STREET

"Fuck that! You think I did that bit so you could sit around here on your skinny little ass hauling in dough night after night? All I understand is that my cut is in someone else's pocket! Probably yours. Now cough it up!"

He stayed cool. "Hey, my man! I don't have your money. I told you, it's all tied up. You can't get to it. And neither can I."

He took a slow drag off his dwindling cigarette, examining the tip as he brought it down from his mouth.

"I want you to think back, Don Roy. Remember, after you left Key West, you scrounged around Vegas for what—two or three years—working these nickel-dime mail order scams and other bullshit routines. You were nowhere till we pulled that diamond sting."

My voice barely contained my rage. "And I was the one who took down the mark."

"*I'm* the one who set that score up, and it took me, like, six or seven months. This was the take of a lifetime, buyo! What do you think, I'm gonna turn over two hundred dimes in cash to you in a brown paper bag so you can run around buying cars and shit? I'm protecting us, you understand? Now if you got a problem with that, take it up with the investment counselor."

15

He went back to his cigarette.

When it came to brass balls, I had to hand it to him. Here I was twice his size, plenty hot, and ready to tear him apart. But he was still jacking with me.

I reached across the desk, grabbing him by his silk shirt.

"Open the safe."

"Hey, what—"

"Open the fucking safe!"

I poised a big fist in front of his face. I saw the beginnings of a quiver. About time.

He got up. I led him by the shirt over to the safe. He opened it, revealing a wad of cash in there, what looked like about seven or eight grand, along with a couple of passports. I took the cash.

"Hey, wait a second! That's—"

"Let's call this the vig," I hissed, shoving him up against the wall. I got right in his face.

"Today's Wednesday. You got one week to come up with my money, the full load. You better know I mean business, Sully. You don't deliver and a couple of Cubans are gonna come calling on you one night, and the next morning you're in the fucking breakfast sausage up in Little Havana. Got it?"

He got it. His fear-filled eyes said so. No more of his cockiness.

SETUP ON FRONT STREET

"Y-yeah, Don Roy. I got it. You'll get the money. You'll get it."

I finally released his shirt with one final push. His back hit the wall.

"Remember, the full load by next Wednesday, or else. And no bullshit stories."

I headed downstairs, out the back door.

The night was still warm but no longer hot. It felt good. Back here behind the building, the Duval Street racket was muffled.

I reached under my guayabera, fingering the scar on my side. I thought about the nigger who shanked me two years ago because I turned the channel on the rec room TV. That's how they do it in there. No warning, no nothing. The minute I turned off his cartoons, he came up behind me and let me have it.

I dropped him in secret last week, just a couple of days before I got processed out.

I had one more stop to make. I decided I would make it, then go back to my nice cool room to watch TV.

Whatever shows I wanted.

THREE

Up the street to Keys Tees, one of a few dozen T-shirt ripoff joints on Duval Street. These places were supposedly owned by various foreign businessmen, mostly Israelis. Keys Tees was no different.

Avi Abraham ran it. I never knew his real name, but whatever it was, you can be sure it was near the top of Israel's Most Wanted list.

Like all the rest of those places, the bright lights inside Keys Tees spilled out to the crowded sidewalk. Hip new music blared its way outside through speakers hanging in the doorway.

The blasting AC dropped the temperature about fifteen degrees as I stepped through the wide-open door. Racks crammed with merchandise crowded the floor. T-shirts covered virtually every square inch of wall space, all of them sporting iron-on decals.

There were no customers, as usual.

SETUP ON FRONT STREET

Nine grand a month rent, with no business on a nice evening in high season? You tell me.

Avi was back at the register, reading a magazine. He never saw me come in.

I hid behind a rack of overpriced tank tops just inside the front door. The music was quieter inside than out on the street.

"Immigration!" I shouted. "Freeze!"

He dropped the magazine as he reflexively jumped off his stool. Quickly, he ducked behind the counter, half-expecting gunfire.

I stepped out into the open, unable to hold back a laugh.

"Hey, nothing to worry about, man. Just tell your Russian bosses you got deported."

Avi slowly straightened up, breaking out into a wide grin as he saw me.

"Donny! Donny! Ah, you're back!" he said in his familiar thick accent. He was the only guy who I let call me Donny.

He came around the counter with open arms and we embraced. I was a little taller than he was, but he was bigger around in the middle. His hair, once jet-black, was now thinning a little, showing slim strips of gray. Dark, expressive eyes threw me a welcome look, and his smile was wide and genuine.

After the hug, with my big shoulders in his small hands, he checked me out, up and down.

"Ah, you look fine, my boy. When did you get out?"

"Three days ago. I just got back in town."

"Must feel good to be back home. Nevada so dry. I been there—Vegas, Reno. I don't like it. Is desert. Like Israel."

"Yeah, except no Israelis."

He laughed. "Is good to see you! So good!"

He finally released my shoulders. A couple of customers wandered in, checking out his selection of Hawaiian shirts. They stayed near the front of the store. He ignored them.

"You know, Donny, things are changing here. Is different from when you left."

"How so?"

"Cuba is going to open up. Very soon. The Soviet Union has disappeared. I'm sure you heard about that." I nodded. "They do not send any more billions of dollars to Castro. He cannot survive without it." I could tell he was getting worked up over this prospect.

He went on. "They say he will be gone by next year, ninety-three at the very latest."

"I've heard about that. What do you care about it?"

"Donny, Donny! We are so close to Cuba. Only ninety miles from Havana itself! When it opens up, we

SETUP ON FRONT STREET

will be a big—how do you say it—point of—of—"

"Jumping-off point," I said.

"Yes, that is it! Jumping-off point. The place where everyone will leave from. You know, everyone will want to go there, it is so beautiful. I have seen it myself. Two years ago, I was in Havana and Varadero. Beautiful beaches, great food, and *ay*! The women! You have never seen such women!"

I tried to calm him down.

"Avi, you forget I was born and raised here. I've been across. I know all about it."

"Ah, yes. Of course. But anyway, the tourist business will multiply here. Double! Triple! Maybe more. Everybody is going to make a lot of money."

"Well," I said, "I'm sure you'll get your share of it." I patted him on the shoulder. "And the Russians'll have to buy bigger gym bags."

I knew the Russian mobsters were drowning in cash since the USSR folded up, and a certain percentage of it was being funneled through places like this one, transported weekly in gym bags from their outpost in Fort Lauderdale.

A quick smile flashed across Avi's face. "So, what can I do for you?"

I caught his eyes narrowing a little. Always the merchant. Getting straight to the point.

I steered him back to the rear counter, away from the customers, lowering my voice to a murmur.

"I need a piece."

His face registered no reaction.

"What kind?"

"Something relatively small. Maybe a .22 semi-auto. With a muffler."

"That is no problem, Donny. For you, anything. Now when do you need it?"

"Tomorrow."

"Tomorrow? So soon. Could be difficult. What time you want it tomorrow?"

He glanced toward the front to see the customers leaving.

"Probably around noon."

"Is very short notice, I don't know..."

Listen to this guy. *"I don't know."*

I fucking knew. I knew he was setting me up. Ex-con out on parole, very risky transaction, very expensive. I could just hear him giving me his line of bullshit.

"Avi, I need it tomorrow. Now can you help me or not?"

"Is not much time, but...well..." Then he grinned again while grabbing my shoulders. "Donny, you come by here at noon tomorrow, I have it for you, okay?"

SETUP ON FRONT STREET

My nod indicated that I appreciated the great effort and sacrifice he was about to make for me.

Another hug and I was out the door.

Duval Street foot traffic was brisk, with lots of cars cruising up and down. I had no doubt Avi would come through for me. I probably could've lined up a weapon somewhere else if I'd been willing to wait, but I wasn't. So I had to go through him.

I don't like doing business with Israelis unless I have to.

But I had a debt to collect, and in my position...well, you get the idea.

FOUR

My bus lag kicked in. I knew I shouldn't't've taken that nap, because I stayed up till way after two.

Despite that, I woke up at seven, just like I'd been forced to do every morning in prison. But I realized I was in a double bed, not a lower bunk. Since I didn't hear any of the usual monkey calls or painful screams, I rolled right over, drifting back to sleep.

By the time I woke up again, it was ten-thirty and I was fine.

Breakfast was at a little egg joint I remembered over on Truman. It was a ways away, but I didn't mind the walk. I wanted to get back into the Key West pace of life.

I took it nice and slow down Elizabeth, a residential street, looking at all the stuff I hadn't seen for so long. The solid houses of Key West's Old Town, each with their own long-held secrets, loomed along both sides of the street all the way to the end.

Lush greenery covered the yards, while occasional splashes of red and peach bougainvillea got all the green up on its feet. People sat rocking on porch chairs beneath slow-turning ceiling fans, while soft radio music flowed here and there through a couple of open windows. A few bicycles gliding up and down the street were the only traffic. The sun promised a long, warm day, and because it was March, there was practically no chance of rain.

My hometown looked good in the late morning. I didn't know how much I'd missed it.

I stopped at a low-hanging frangipani tree, then tugged at one of the limbs, pulling the soft pink buds to my nose. The fragrance was overpowering, sending me back six or seven years, right before I left for Vegas. Back to Norma, back to all those promises we made to each other, back to when her perfumed hair would make me dizzy, when I kissed her for the last time...

Norma...Norma...

***

After breakfast, I stepped out of the eatery into the heat. In only about one hour, the temperature had shot right up—it'll do that here. As I moved along Truman toward downtown, tiny rivulets of sweat broke out along the back of my neck.

Duval Street at noon. A regular fucking circus.

The college crowd was in town for spring break, with the boys riding shirtless up and down the street on their rented mopeds, swerving, beeping, whooping. Behind them on the moped seats, girls in bikinis clung to their waists, probably looking forward to an afternoon of Jello shots.

I was glad when I finally got to Keys Tees because I knew the AC would cool me down fast. It did, while I took note of the eight or ten customers browsing around different parts of the store.

Cruise ship passenger types, all of them. A couple of Avi's relatives worked the floor: a foxy girl with flowing black hair and a slim young guy with the required beard stubble spoke to the suckers in accented English, pushing them to buy decals for their shirts, which would conveniently jack up the price by about triple.

Whoever dreamed up this racket was a stone genius.

A tall, rawboned guy with a yellow crewcut came out of the back, definitely not Israeli, but Avi followed him out as far as the counter. I made him as a Russian.

He carried a gym bag which, by the way it swung

in his grip, looked empty. He left without any goodbyes. Avi saw me, then beckoned me to the back.

The back room was a hodgepodge of clutter. Clothing all over the place, on hangers, in boxes, on shelves, on the floor, even piled up on the folding picnic table along the side wall. The table served as a desk, while somewhere underneath all of the T-shirts was a telephone along with other office-type shit.

Avi pushed some of the clothes aside as we took seats in the plastic chairs at the table. Sidelong, I glimpsed the safe, thinking about the Russian and the empty gym bag. It must've been cash delivery day.

A Burger King sack sat on the table behind a pile of T-shirts. Avi pulled it toward himself, simultaneously reaching inside. From under the french fries, he pulled a Browning .22 semiautomatic.

"They don't get colder than this, Donny," he said under his breath. "Never been fired."

He held it gingerly in both hands, like it was a jar of nitro about to go off, while his small, black eyes constantly darted over his shoulder.

Taking it from him, I looked it over. It looked good. I jacked the slide, noting the smooth and easy feel. It had good balance to it, and was nice and light.

"Ammo?"

"Yes, of course."

He reached back in the bag and pulled out two full clips along with a box of shells and a silencer, all wrapped in a Burger King wrapper.

I loaded the gun and put the extra clip in my pocket. I rewrapped the silencer and the shell box, returning it to the bag under the Whopper. The heater went into my rear waistband.

"How much?"

"Donny, you know is very hard to get a—a virgin piece like this one. And you want it so quickly. I had to call my—"

"Skip the bullshit, Avi. How much?"

"Normally, I would charge fifteen hundred, Donny, because you know is crime to sell gun to a convicted felon. But for you, I make it one thousand even."

What a crock of shit. He could've gotten a surface-to-air missile launcher if I'd wanted one, and in half the time. As it was, he probably got the .22 for free from the Russian who just left, so now he wants me to pour on the gravy.

Fuck it.

The bazaar was now open.

"Four hundred," I said. "That's all it's worth."

"Four hundred? Donny, this is a fine weapon, never been fired. It cost me more than that. I can maybe go down to eight-fifty. But no lower."

"Shit, for eight-fifty I could buy two of these anywhere else. Plus a couple of hundred rounds to go with them. I'll give you five because you got it for me overnight."

"Donny, please. I take big chance selling you this gun. I could go to prison. My business would close! My family—"

"Okay, okay, spare me the tears. Five-fifty and that's it. And before you say yes, I want you to remember who it was back in eighty-four who shook down the owner of that building in the next block. Remember? When he swore he'd never sell it to you people? And now you own it, right? And what do you suppose is in that building right now? One of your T-shirt operations! Can you say 'thank you'?"

"All right, Donny," he sighed, looking downcast. "Five-fifty. But I paid you to do that job."

"Yeah, yeah, I know."

He did pay me for that job, all right. Ten thousand, in fact, so the owner would cave and sell him the building for three hundred big ones, about twice what it was worth. Everybody made out on the deal. Me, the owner, but especially Avi and the Russians, who are now running millions through that location.

As I reached into my pocket, I carefully pulled out just a few of the C-notes I glommed off Sully last night.

I didn't want Avi to know I was quite so flush. Once the mini-roll was in plain sight, I peeled off six while I fanned out the rest, making sure he saw I only had three or four left. He pulled fifty change out of his own pocket, mumbling some comment about being careful.

I put the burger bag under my arm and split.

FIVE

City Hall was in the same building as the police station, on Angela Street, just a few doors up from my rooming house. Even though I'd stashed the hardware back in my room where no one could find it, I was plenty nervous going in there. It crawled with cops. I had to thread my way through all of them to get to the mayor's office on the second floor.

There it was at the end of the hall. The sign on the door said "Wilson J Whitney Jr, Mayor".

Wilson J Whitney, Junior.

Boy King.

It was lunchtime, so no receptionist. I walked in without knocking.

He was on the phone, relaxed, leaning back in his swivel chair. When he saw me, he jolted into a straight-up facing-front position.

"Yeah, that's right," he said into the telephone, in a

let's-get-this-over-with kind of tone. "Boston for a nickel. Right...right. Okay...later."

He came out from behind his desk. He'd always been short, a little on the slim side, but he'd gained weight since I'd last seen him. He'd kept most of his good looks along with most of his sandy hair, a thatch of which perpetually dangled over his forehead.

As he pasted on his best campaign grin, he stuck out his hand.

"Well, as I live and breathe. Don Roy Doyle! Welcome home, bubba."

He pulled me into a phony embrace, patting me across the shoulders.

"I heard you were back. When'd you get in town?"

He heard I was back. You can see what a job it is to keep a low profile in this burg.

"Yesterday."

I pulled away before he could.

"Care for a little refreshment?" He gestured toward the small wet bar in the corner.

"No thanks."

"Well, I'm gonna have one." He patted his stomach. "I just had an early lunch at El Siboney, and every time I have Cuban food, I need a little taste to help with my digestion."

He poured a healthy shot of Bacardi over rocks,

then splashed it with Coke. I had a strong hunch that he took this digestive aid after every meal, regardless of its ethnic origin.

He took a pretty good pull on the drink. I tried a little small talk.

"So you finally made mayor."

"Well, when you left for Las Vegas, let's see, it was what, seven or eight years ago? I'd just come back from up in Tallahassee as Senator Roberts' assistant. Not long after that, I was elected to the City Commission. Then mayor in eighty-nine. My first of what I hope will be several terms."

I was sure it would be. Everyone in town was sure.

He was just one of those people, you know, predestined for all this, starting with his student council election when we were at Key West High. That's where he picked up the Boy King handle.

His father had been mayor since before I could remember, and everyone just knew that BK would follow the same trail. He went away to college—Florida State, I think. That's where they all go. Then he got his first cushy political job.

Now he's right where everyone knew he would be. Where he belonged, you might say.

"Did I hear you say Boston just now?" I asked. "As in Celtics?"

He chuckled.

"Just a friendly wager on tonight's game."

I chuckled back.

BK'd been making these "friendly wagers" since I ran my football pool back in high school. He couldn't pick any winners then, either.

"Five hundred dollars sounds pretty friendly. Who else you got?"

He turned coy. "It's not who else do I have, but what else is on your mind, Don Roy?"

"Norma."

He clasped his hands together as he rocked back in his chair.

"Yeah, Norma. Well, you, uh, came to the wrong place. I don't have any idea where she is."

"When I left for Vegas, you had a pretty good idea."

"It was all over between you two before you left. You know that, don't you? You'd run out of hustles here on the island so you went where the money was. You couldn't afford to take her with you and she knew it. Before you could cut her loose, she came to me. What can I say?"

He shrugged his shoulders.

His youthful look hadn't yet left him, even though he was around my age. That was one of his tools he used to get what he wanted. The wide eyes, the raised brows, the whole innocent choirboy routine. He had it down cold, and it made a lot of people cozy up to him.

Of course, they were always unaware of the knife that he was usually plunging into their backs.

Politics. You can have it.

So here he was, running his game on me, as though he'd had nothing to do with Norma's dumping me, as though she'd conveniently fallen out of the sky into his lap. Headfirst, no doubt.

All without his wife knowing about it.

He took another swallow of rum and Coke, then swayed the glass from side to side, clinking the ice.

I wanted to reach over and slap him upside the head. Him and his fucking drink.

But I knew better.

You don't muscle the mayor in this town. Especially when you're fresh out of the joint.

I looked around the office for a few seconds, as though I'd accepted his line. Then I turned back to him, locking my eyes onto his.

"So where is she, BK?"

"I told you, I don't know. We split up around a year ago."

He knew. I just didn't dare pound it out of him.

"Where is she? Still in town?"

He shifted in his chair. "I don't know. I just don't

know where you can find her. She might've left the island."

He downed the last of his drink, then got up from his chair.

"Now, you're gonna have to excuse me, Don Roy. I've got a meeting in a couple of minutes."

"Yeah, well, if you can manage to remember where she might be, or if by some long shot, you just happen to remember her phone number, tell her to find me. I'll be around."

I took a pen off his desk, then wrote the number of my rooming house on a piece of note paper. I tossed the number back on his desk along with the pen.

He looked at it. "Where are you staying now? What about your mother's house up there on—where was it—Packer Street?"

"It went for taxes after she died."

He started walking me to the door.

"That's a goddamn shame, bubba. You grow up in a nice little house in a friendly neighborhood, live there all your life, and then they snatch it up for taxes. That's happened to a lot of good people here. They wind up moving way up to Ocala where they can afford a decent place to live. You know, we've actually lowered property taxes here since I've been in office. Trying to prevent just that kind of thing from happening."

SETUP ON FRONT STREET

His arm snaked around my shoulder as we got to the door. Right on cue.

"If I'm re-elected, I'm gonna lower 'em again, or die trying, I swear. And pretty soon, when Cuba opens up, there's gonna be plenty of money to go around, so it'll be easier to lower the taxes."

Ever notice how these politicians are all alike? You know, how they'll do anything, anything at all, to get your vote. It's like they're all the same person, just with different skins.

I didn't want to remind him that I couldn't vote. And that if I could, I wouldn't.

***

As I made my way to the front of the building, a hand grabbed my shoulder hard from behind. Without looking, I slapped it away, wheeling around instinctively in an attack posture.

I didn't like what I saw.

"Whoa-ho, big man. Better not try it. You're in civilization now."

"You could've fooled me, Ortega."

"I heard you got back in town. Things are a little different around here now."

I looked straight at him. He was about ten years

37

younger than me, in pretty good shape, but not quite as big. The only thing different-looking was that he was in street clothes. I hoped he'd been fired. No police force needs an asshole like him.

I turned away, heading for the door.

He followed me outside and when we reached the top of the steps, he grabbed me again, this time by the arm. When he spun me around, it was all I could do to contain myself.

"I said things are different now." Attitude dripped out of his wiseass smirk.

"I heard you the first time."

My narrowed eyes told him to back off.

"As you can see, I'm no longer in uniform. I made detective."

"When are they gonna put your statue out front?"

"Very funny. Look, dickhead, you better walk right from now on. You make even one tiny slipup and I'll violate your ass right back to the joint. And when I do, they may not put up a statue, but they'll probably give me a fucking commendation. And a gold watch to go with it."

"Listen, Ortega —"

"*Detective* Ortega to you, scumbag."

"Detective Ortega..."

I really shouldn't've had to endure all this so soon

after getting out. It was hard to hold it in. I mean, if anyone had done this to me just a few days ago, while I was still inside, they'd be lying on the floor right now, swallowing their own blood.

But standing there on the top step of the City Hall building, with people coming and going all around me, and with the entire city police force just a few feet inside the door, I just gritted my teeth.

"I haven't done anything and you know it."

"Yeah, not yet, maybe. But sooner or later you will. And when you do..."

He ground his fist hard into his palm in an attempt to scare me to death.

"I can't believe you've still got this hair up your ass," I told him. "All because I beat the shit out of your big brother ten years ago and ruined your hero worship. I don't suppose you'd want to know what really happened. Like him coming at me with a broken bottle."

"Shut the fuck up!"

He poked my chest with a stiff index finger.

That's when I really had to suck it up. You see, according to prison protocol, when another inmate does that to you, they're telling you that the all-out attack is on its way, coming right now. At that point, your job is to get in the first blow right then and there, no matter how big the guy is.

All my reflexes told me to unload on him right then, and I came real close.

Instead, I slowly reached into my pants pocket for a pair of red dice.

I began grinding them together in my closed fist to relieve the tension. Otherwise I was going to explode. I'd seen Humphrey Bogart do the same thing once in a movie, only he had these little round steel balls. It looked like it worked for him, so I tried it a couple of years ago. It felt good since it usually relieved the tension all right, but when violence became unavoidable, the dice in my fist added authority to my punch.

Ortega's nostrils flared, his eyes burning with fury.

"I've busted a thousand lowlife punks like you! All thinking they're the baddest, downest motherfuckers on the block. And you're no different. Pretty soon, you'll be back to your old ways, looking for angles. And when you find one..." His voice lowered and his upper lip raised into a sneer. "Well, guess who's gonna be right there with the cuffs."

I felt I was going to crush the dice into powder.

"Excuse me while I piss in my pants."

He turned to go back in the building. "Just remember. I'll be watching. And waiting." He pointed that index finger at my face. "One slip and you're back inside."

MIKE DENNIS

SIX

That night found me in Mambo's. My hangout long before I left town. The only place I really ever felt comfortable.

It was a dim little spot with no sign out front, nestled on one of the Old Town side streets, a block or so off Truman. Most of its small clientele usually operated on the wrong side of the law. Its chief activity was Mambo's bolita game and sports book run out of the back room. Because he kept all the right palms greased, he did good business.

The food was by far the tastiest Cuban fare in all of the Keys, but we were the only ones who could get it. Citizen customers were discouraged from entering. Mambo didn't need any outsiders hanging around. Those who did wander in were treated rudely by the Cuban "waiter", if they got any service at all.

They never returned.

SETUP ON FRONT STREET

***

I had polished off the last of my picadillo when he came to my booth. I got up and we hugged.

"Don Roy. *¿Cómo estás, mi hermano?*" His upper body was still rock-solid, even though I made him to be crowding sixty.

"*Bien, bien.* Now that I'm back home, it's all great."

He was one of the few guys I looked forward to seeing when I got out. Being from the DeLima family made him a pretty right guy to have on your side.

The DeLimas weren't gangsters or anything, not in the traditional sense, anyway. But it was well-known that you didn't do anything to piss them off. They'd been on the island for over a hundred and fifty years and their interests penetrated into every segment of Key West life.

He took the seat across from me, then pulled out a fresh Cohiba and unwrapped it. He ran the length of it past his nose for a moment, and from the slight smile that cracked his face, you'd think he just entered heaven. Snipping off the tip, he reached for his lighter.

"How's the food?" he asked in Spanish. "As good as you remember?" He took his time lighting the cigar.

Fortunately, my Spanish chops were still high. Growing up here, you have a choice. Learn Spanish or

43

ignore it at your own risk. I learned it, mostly on the streets. And since the Nevada prison held a lot of Mexicans, I heard it every day while I was gone.

But it was different out there—the Spanish, I mean. The accent, the rhythm and everything, it was all different, and I didn't like the Mexicans at all.

They were a well-organized, pushy bunch who controlled all the dope coming into the joint. They were always fighting with the niggers over one thing or another, so I tried to stay out of their way.

Even still, I had a few run-ins with them—I even had to ice one of them about a year ago—but I fell into the Spanish pretty quick. You know what they say, use it or lose it.

"La mejor comida que he tenido en años," I said.

I frankly surprised myself at how easily the Cuban Spanish came back to me. My accent was nearly flawless, as it had been before I left.

My eyes swept the room. A few guys sat at the bar watching the basketball game. From what I could tell, the Celtics were getting killed. A salsa tune poured out of the overhead speakers. A pool shark I knew had apparently reeled someone into a game of nine-ball. Anxious onlookers surrounded the table, changing money after every shot.

I looked into Mambo's warm eyes. "I've really

missed it here, brother."

"We've missed you too, man."

He twirled the cigar in his mouth, drawing deep pleasure from it while slowly blowing a column of heavy smoke toward the ceiling. Normally, I hate those fucking cigars—they're just so damned nasty—but this one sweetened the air somehow. When you combined it with the tangy aroma of Cuban food drifting out of the kitchen, it was sort of like the warm breath of chocolate spreading itself over that dank joint.

He told me, "You know, you gained a lot of respect around here standing up the way you did. Taking the rap for Sullivan and keeping your mouth shut."

I shrugged.

He went on. "How are you fixed, brother?"

I could see him reaching into his pocket. I motioned palms down a couple of times, a forget-it gesture.

"*Todo está bien*. I got a stake. And I'm expecting big things in about a week."

As the waiter came by to scoop up my plate, I saw my empty glass. "But I would like another beer."

"Eduardo," he said. "*¡Dos cervezas!*"

Within seconds, two fresh cold ones sat in front of us. I slowly drank from mine to wash down the rib-sticking meal.

The basketball game ended on TV. The Celtics went

down by twenty-five points.

I said to Mambo through a chuckle, "You know, I was in BK's office today and I heard him on the phone betting a nickel on the Celtics."

"That stupid asshole. He bet it with me. He had Portland, too. Another loser. A fast thousand in my pocket."

I laughed. Then out of curiosity, I asked him, "Does he bet with you all the time?"

"Every day," he replied. "At least seven, eight hundred a day."

I went for another cold pull from the beer. "I remember when I had my football pool back in high school, he bet with me every week and lost his ass for four years."

"Well, he's still losing his ass. He's dumping about three grand a week now, sometimes more. You know, I have players who want to know the teams he's betting on so they can take the opponents. That's how much faith they have in him, picking winners."

We laughed and drank to it.

Mambo pushed a leathery hand through his still-thick hair. Gray had taken it over, as it was about to do with mine. He'd put on a little weight, although his shoulders were still hard. Black eyes peered intensely over high cheekbones and a prominent mouth, giving him a strong presence.

His smile slipped away. "So, did they treat you okay out there? *¿Tuviste problemas?*"

"I had a few problems. Nothing I couldn't handle."

He didn't press me for the gory details. He knew better.

Instead he changed the subject, which brought his smile back.

"You know, Pepe Santiago made it to the majors. He's playing for the Pirates right now. We're all so proud of him."

I smiled, too. Pepe was a real badass kid—quit school early, started pulling bullshit stickups, dealing drugs, the whole stupid shot. When I left town, he was around seventeen. He hadn't been caught yet, but believe me, he didn't have a prayer. He was on the big night train, looking hard for that bullet with his name on it.

While he was still in school, however, he was a great baseball player. Gifted with supple infielder's hands and all the quick moves.

"That's terrific," I said. "How'd that happen?"

"Coach García got to him. He couldn't convince Pepe to come back to school and play for the Conchs, but one spring he took him up to Miami to an open tryout the Pirates were having. Pepe got out there and showed why he was the best shortstop ever to play for the Conchs. They offered him a contract, and three or four years later, he was in the big show. He's a starter now."

It didn't really surprise me. Before I split town, I always followed the local team. Pepe was just coming into his own before he quit school.

Baseball is big here. It's played every day of the year in one form or another, but at the high school level—the Key West Conchs—it becomes deadly serious. The team always ranks high nationally, winning a lot of state championships. Big league scouts make routine trips down here to check out the new talent. If you've got Coach García on your side, you've got big juice. When he walks into a major league tryout touting you as a prospect, they take a look.

I was glad to hear that Pepe got a break because he deserved it. I knew his family. They were good people.

I digested that good news as Mambo and I took a couple more sips of beer.

The nearby pool game ended abruptly with an unlikely shot, the winner whooping in excitement, and money furiously changing hands among the spectators.

Mambo puffed on his cigar again, then brought it down to table level. He leaned slightly forward, softening his posture.

SETUP ON FRONT STREET

"*Mi hermano, tú sabes...que ella todavía está aquí en el cayo.*"

I was right in the middle of swallowing. The beer went down hard. Our eyes bonded.

He didn't wait for me to say anything. He didn't speak her name. He didn't have to. All he had to do was tell me she was still on the island. I knew who he meant.

He added, "She's working at the Fun House."

"The Fun House?"

"That's a new place. Opened after you left. It's a massage parlor up the other end of Duval Street."

"Massage parlor?" My fists clenched.

"*Yo sé, hombre, yo sé.* But I'm just telling you, you know? That's where she works."

"What—how did she wind up there?"

He reached across the table to put his hands on mine.

"Man, I don't know the whole story. I just know that she was working there for a while before BK dumped her." He squeezed my hands. "I'm really sorry. *Lo siento mucho.*"

A new nine-ball game had started up, complete with yammering bettors. The overhead speakers pushed out more salsa. Over the music, frenzied TV announcers rehashed the blowout of the Celtics.

But all I could hear were Mambo's quiet words.

SEVEN

The Fun House was up at the artsy-fartsy end of Duval with all the art galleries and whatnot, away from all the bars and the tourists. Kind of hidden down this little alley behind a vacant storefront. No sign on the door, of course.

The walk downtown took me twenty hard minutes. My brain raced in fourth gear all the way, trying to figure out how I wanted to handle this whole thing. I played out various scenarios in my mind, but they all ended in flames. It was just that I never had to deal with anything like this before, you know?

Shit, this was *Norma*, for Chrissake. *Norma!*

By the time I stepped through the flimsy Fun House door, I still didn't know what I would say to her.

The girl at the desk wore too much makeup. Her lipstick made a shapeless red blob on her pinched face. It all stuck out beneath a badly-teased haystack of hair.

51

That's not to say that more careful attention would've improved her appearance.

She waved her hands around as she spoke. Chipped blue nail polish distracted my attention while she ran through all the prelims, telling me I was only paying for a massage in private, nothing illegal was happening, was I a cop, and on and on.

When she asked me if there was a particular girl I wanted, I said Norma.

"Norma? I don't think we have a Norma here."

"She's here. That's who I want."

"Well, there's nobody here by that name, but let's see."

She turned toward the back room, calling out the available girls. Three of them stepped lazily through the cheap gold curtain.

There she was.

She gasped as she saw me. I made a soft gesture toward her. The other two disappeared back where they came from.

The girl at the desk said, "Oh, you want Candy." I nodded as she asked, "Will that be cash or charge?"

I peeled off a bill without taking my eyes off Norma. Finally, we went to a small room off the hallway in the back. She closed the door behind us.

The bed took up most of the room. We just stood

there for a moment looking at each other, comparing recall to reality.

It wasn't easy, because the only light in the room came from a small low-wattage lamp on the bedside table. It cast a distorting yellowish glare over the immediate area, fading to dimness. The window AC strained to cool things down, but all it really did was make a lot of noise. A slight odor of mildew hung over everything.

Her eyes, once a lively and crisp blue, were now washed out, nearly colorless, encircled by thick mascara and dark brows. Her face was never what you would call beautiful — her nose and mouth were way too small, if you know what I mean — so she didn't hit most people as sexy. A lot of hard times showed on that face right now, and her shoulders sagged under the strain.

I noticed her hair. It still held the beautiful light brown of my memory, but it was messy and looked like shit. Her mouth, so often lit by what I thought to be a pretty smile, now drooped downward at the corners, carved with permanent creases. I'd seen the same defeated look on hundreds of faces in the pen.

I hated to admit this, but her figure was starting to slip, too. I mean, I know she was about thirty-eight, so you have to expect some concessions here and there.

53

You can't stay young and fresh forever. But this didn't look like any battle with Father Time. It looked more like she'd neglected herself for a while now.

I took her pale, petite hand in both of mine.

"What happened?" I barely got it out.

She looked away.

With her hand still in mine, I reached up under her chin, gently tilting her head back toward me. My eyes repeated the question.

Again she turned her head. I gave her a lot of time, so she took it.

Finally, she said, "I needed the money."

"Needed the money? What for? What happened to your job?"

Her eyes were now on the floor, while her voice dripped sarcasm. "My job? Which one?"

"Well, back when you were working at the Raw Bar."

"Ha! Sure! The Raw Bar. Slinging beer and oysters. Good for two or three hundred a week."

"So—so what happened? I mean, it was good enough back then. What the hell happened?"

"I didn't want to go on working there my whole life. That's what happened."

She looked back up at me, right through my eyes and straight into my head, where she'd always, always been.

"I wanted...I wanted to make money. To have the things I never had. I didn't want to have to scrounge for the rest of my life."

"And you don't think you could get those things working a respectable job?"

"Respectable job? Look who's talking. When was the last time *you* drew an honest day's pay?"

"Okay, okay, but you know what I mean. Did you have to...to do *this* just so you could buy yourself things? I mean, couldn't you have taken a second job or...or something?"

Her eyes turned downward again.

"I needed more. A lot more."

I stiffened at those code words. Now I was sure, absolutely sure, that somewhere in there was white powder and a straw, or maybe a needle.

"Tell me, honey. Please tell me." I steeled myself.

"I can't. I just can't!" Tears found their way onto her face.

I sat us both down on the bed.

"Yes, you can."

I softly stroked her cheek, then dabbed at her tears with a tissue from the table, not wanting to smear her caked-on makeup.

"Now, go ahead."

"Oh, Don Roy, I can't! You'll never forgive me. You probably still hate me for the way I left you, and I just *know* you'll never forgive me for...for all this."

She swept the squalid little room with an arm gesture. I saw more tears dribbling out.

More tissue, more dabbing.

"Listen, honey, I don't hate you and I never will. Now, just take it nice and slow. Start from the beginning."

She sobbed out loud, burying her head in my chest.

I could tell she was ashamed of where she went with her life. Both my arms wrapped around her. I didn't even think about it, I just did it.

At last, I held her again, her familiar shape and form contoured to mine, even in that awkward position there on that squeaky bed. The first time in nearly seven years, but for just a second there, it felt like all that time never passed, or somehow melted away.

Even though she was crying, I felt joy just having her so close. No matter what happened after tonight, I knew that this moment would be a snapshot I would carry with me my whole life.

I prompted her again to tell me. She got it together and started to speak.

"I started doing this..." She sniffled and swallowed. "I started doing this to...to...get money for BK."

SETUP ON FRONT STREET

I heard the words but wanted to think I didn't. I wanted to think the rumbling AC drowned them out.

"*What?*"

"It was all to get money for BK."

My arms released her from my tender embrace. My big hands shook her shoulders instead.

"What in the *fuck* are you talking about?"

Her voice was still full of tears. "See? I told you you wouldn't forgive me. I...I..."

Right then, I didn't know what to do, whether to be pissed off or gently understanding. Actually, I was both, but I just didn't know how to show it.

I shook her shoulders again, and I tried to say "What?", but my voice wasn't working.

"He...he...needed a lot of money to...to pay off his gambling debts. He owed, like, thousands."

"What the — what — "

None of this was computing. The truth was, I didn't want it to.

You know, when you hear shit like this, you don't want it to go any farther. You really wish it could somehow back itself up into its stinking black hole as though you'd never heard it in the first place.

But of course, once it's out, it's like the genie. There's no stuffing it back inside.

"You'd been gone from here for a few years

already. I think it was right after you got sent up. He and I were already seeing each other, you know. Then he got way behind in his gambling debts, you know, betting on games and stuff. Some of Mambo's men threatened to hurt him bad. Oh, Don Roy, I was there that night. It was terrible! They — the things they said they'd do — "

"Wait a second! BK's been gambling since we were in high school. He's always paid his debts. He never needed money! Shit, the Whitneys are one of the richest families in town! Why, when the old man was mayor, he stole more fucking money than they could print! What — why — "

She sniffled a couple of times. "Well, one day the old man turned the faucet off. I guess he got tired of making good on BK's debts. Said if he needed to pay Mambo off he was gonna have to get the money from somewhere else. He thought it would get BK to stop gambling."

"So..."

"He didn't make me, no, if that's what you're thinking. But he did suggest it. Like it was the only way to come up with cash real quick. I mean, he was only a city commissioner then, and you know, they don't get paid shit. And he owed Mambo about nine thousand dollars. Mambo'd been carrying him for a few weeks."

"He *suggested* that you...you do this?"

"He was desperate! They were gonna break his legs, or maybe kill him! You know Mambo. He doesn't screw around!"

"But he told you to sell yourself? So you could pay off *his debts*?"

The room almost started to spin. I really couldn't take this.

"He didn't tell me to. I agreed to do it. I cared about him, you know? And it was only gonna be for a little while, until he could get straight with Mambo."

She reached for another couple of tissues, then wiped her nose. Outside I heard distant thunder. It surprised me. We were still a couple of months from rainy season.

"Besides, he said he loved me. Said he was gonna leave Rita."

"Leave Rita?" I had to laugh. "You know how long they've been married? He'd never leave her."

Not that he'd never leave her, mind you, only that he'd never leave her for Norma, but I didn't want to say that.

You see, Norma didn't realize that people like BK and Rita lived way up there, operating in their own little gold-plated world with others just like them, drinking champagne and shit, doing whatever the hell they wanted.

All the while, people like her and me scrounged around down here, close to the zero, fighting for their scraps while taking their shit our whole lives.

"Well, he said he was going to leave her. For me. And he said he was gonna do it right after he won the mayor's election. If I could only help him out of his jam."

"And you fucking *did* it? You started selling your ass for that motherfucker? To pay off his markers?"

No matter how hard I tried, and I *was* trying, I just couldn't bring myself to believe this.

"I told you, it was only supposed to be temporary. And after about two months, I'd given him the nine thousand plus about another four in interest."

I groaned.

"Don't tell me. After he squared himself with Mambo, he kept on betting and losing."

"Right, and he—"

"Sure! Because he had you to cover his goddam losses. And you kept on fucking God knows how many guys a night just to keep him in action!"

My gut churned with rage. It really hurt. I was close to puking it all up in one big industrial-strength retch.

Her eyes burst with shame as her head plowed into

—

my chest again, sobbing loudly.

"Yes. Yes. That's right!" Tears continued streaming down her cheeks. "And then he threatened to break it off."

"Why?"

It thundered again, this time a little louder.

"After he was elected in, I think, eighty-nine, then he said he wanted to wait till this year, when he would get *re*-elected. He said after that, he'd be unbeatable for all time, and then he could leave Rita with no problem."

She crumpled up the tissue and glanced around for a wastebasket. I took it from her soft hand and tossed it on the floor.

She continued. "But then about a year ago, she found out about us. She warned him she was gonna go public with it. And that would've ruined his re-election chances. He wants to be mayor so bad, you know, to serve the people..."

"Yeah, right. But you're still with him?"

"Well, yeah. Just...just not as often as I used to be."

"What do you mean?"

She shifted her weight on the bed and crossed her legs.

"We used to see each other a lot, you know, like two or three times a week. This was right after you left and I was so alone and..."

"I know, honey. Go on."

"Anyway, we stayed like that for a long time until Rita found out about us. Now we don't see each other too often. He comes around once a week for the money and then—"

"He comes around here to collect your money?"

I reached for the dice in my pocket. I ground them together with as much fury as my hand could muster.

"Yeah. But we actually spend time together about once every two or three weeks. He swears, though, that we'll..."

I put an index finger to her lips.

"Norma, listen. He's lying scum. Outside of the money, he doesn't give a shit for you. He's got you in here..." I covered the room with a hand gesture.

"Don Roy," she said, "you don't understand. I mean, I've been doing this for three years now." Her voice was flat, in a scary kind of way, and her reddened eyes came up to meet mine. "The first two years were all for BK. Now I'm doing it for myself. I'm making good money and instead of giving it all to him, I get to keep most of it."

"What do you mean by good money?"

The thunder moved closer. I heard rain tapping the roof.

"About eighteen hundred a week. I still give BK a

little, `cause he's still gambling and he needs it."

"You *still* cover his losses? How much?"

"Not all of them. I only give him about eight or nine hundred a week, sometimes more. He actually loses more, but I don't give it to him. I think he's got some way of stealing the rest of it from the city. But sometimes I don't give him anything at all. Those are the weeks he wins. Baseball season is coming up and he can pick those games pretty good."

"Oh yeah, BK's just a regular champ at picking baseball winners."

She twitched a little. "But it's not like before, I told you. I get to keep a lot for myself. Sometimes as much as a thousand a week."

I groaned again.

She went on: "Most of the girls make a lot more than that, but they're a lot younger'n I am and they get the best customers." She'd calmed herself by now, while I unraveled. "Plus," she added, "I get to control the men for a change, instead of the other way around."

My mind reeled. Norma...my Norma. I swear, if BK had been in that room with us, I'd've taken him out right then and there, no questions asked.

She moved around again on the bed but her cheap polyester dress didn't move with her, clinging to her in all the wrong places. She adjusted it a little, then straightened up.

"You remember I told you what it was like with my first husband?" she said. "All the time hitting me and everything. And then my second one, you know, a real control freak. Mind games all the damn time, till I went damn near crazy. And my father before them."

"But *I* never treated you that way."

"No, you didn't."

A sweet hand went up to my cheek, caressing it. For just a moment, love sparkled in those faded blue eyes, hypnotic love. And all the rage in me fell away, just like that.

"You was always real good to me, and I never forgot it. You was really the only man ever treated me right."

I softened about as much as possible. "So why...why don't you just tell BK to shove it?"

"You've been gone a long time, Don Roy. I really didn't think you were ever coming back. And like I said, I can't make this kind of money waitressing."

I groped for words. "Yeah, but—but you—"

"When you left, remember, I was living in that shit trailer over on Stock Island. Remember? Scumbags and drug dealers everywhere? I was afraid to step outside. You remember that? Well, now I've got my own apartment at Ocean Walk, that new complex up on

South Roosevelt. It's a great place and I'm paying for it myself."

I still choked on the words. They wouldn't come.

She said, "I've got a real nice car, too. A Toyota. I mean, I didn't get it new—it's an '88—but it looks real nice. More important, I saved up and paid cash for it. So it's all *mine*. You know what that means to me, Don Roy? To pay cash for a nice car?"

Yeah, I knew. The first time I'd done it, it meant a lot to me, too.

"Listen, Norma..."

I swallowed hard, struggling to find the right words. They had to be just right or else, because I only had one shot at saying them. I took a long breath.

"Right now, you might think you like this shit. You're pulling in a dime a week and paying your rent."

She inhaled so I could hear it, getting ready to interrupt with a lot of bullshit about how she could do this as long as she wanted.

I shushed her. "Just let me finish. You've been in the business long enough now to know what every hooker knows: that somewhere out there is that one wacked-out psycho who's looking to cut you up or to strangle the life out of you, and you're hoping he never finds you. Or at the very least, that he gets off on doing it to someone else before he gets around to you."

"That's not going to happen. Not here."

"You say that now. But let me tell you, if that ever did happen, I could *never* live with myself, knowing that I had this one opportunity right now to get you out of this racket once and for all. So...I'm asking you to quit. To come with me and be my woman. And let me be your man."

"But my—"

Another index finger to her lips.

"Money won't be a problem. I'm getting a big windfall—call it an inheritance—next week. I'm talking major money. We can take it and live like human beings. We can even leave the island if you want to."

I pulled her close to me. Right up on my chest again with my arms all the way around her.

"Norma, don't you see? This is what I've always wanted. What I waited for the last three years I spent out there in hell. You wouldn't believe the shit I put up with waiting for this day. I forgive you, I forgive you everything. Please say you'll do it."

"Oh, Don Roy, I...I..."

She moved her head to look up at me, locking my eyes into hers. "I've always hoped you'd come back to me. Do you really mean all that?"

"You know I do, honey."

"Then, yes. Yes. I'll do it. Because I love you, baby. I

love you so much. Yes! I'll do it! I'll quit. For you. For us."

I held her so tight, burying my face in her hair.

Beneath the Walgreen's perfume, I caught a whiff of her natural human scent. I'd never forgotten it. It made me high as I breathed it in deep. It swelled my nostrils, stirred my loins, gentle as a tropical breeze.

But more powerful than a September hurricane.

"As of this moment," I whispered, "you're free of BK. I'll see to it."

She squeezed me as hard as she could. We lay down together, and as I gathered her in my arms, great sheets of rain slapped the tin roof to a rolling clap of thunder. Very rare for this time of year.

EIGHT

It rained most of the night. I was up and showered early, then out into the cool, wet street at about quarter of eight.

I didn't know what time BK arrived at his office, but I knew he wouldn't be there yet. I wanted to see him before he walked in.

You want to talk serious shit to a big shot, especially if it involves an underlying threat, you don't do it in his office if you can help it. That's his turf.

He's the one sitting behind the big desk with all the phones and the switches and everything at his fingertips, while everybody's kissing his ass. In there he's king shit. He feels like you can't touch him, and in a way, he's right.

But out in the street or in a parking lot, when he's on his way to the throneroom, he's just another square moe going to work. Out here, he's still vulnerable and he knows it. This is my turf, this in-between zone where I could hammer my point home in full stereo.

I went to the city garage where I waited across from his parking spot.

I skipped breakfast; eating would take the edge off. But as I stood around in the damp concrete structure, I felt a sharp desire for a cigarette. It was the kind of pang I used to have back in the joint when I was trying to quit. It promised me that if I grabbed that one smoke, then I could really stay quit afterward.

You know, the tension, the stress, that builds on you in prison day after day is tremendous. The strain piles up on you, no matter what. You've got to find some way of working through it, of relieving it, or else you don't make it in there.

I tried a lot of things. I lifted weights, I read a lot, anything to take my mind off it. A lot of times I wanted to light one up just to ease the load, it was so damn heavy. I only wanted one cigarette then, like I do right now.

Just one.

But I couldn't leave to go buy any because I didn't want to miss BK, so I beat back the craving.

Finally, about nine-thirty, his Dodge came sloshing through the garage entrance. He slid into his spot and got out without seeing me.

"BK," I called out as I approached him.

He turned. He was not pleased with what he saw: that's right, me again. He dragged out his standard smile anyway, taping it onto his face.

"Don Roy, what's up?"

"Let's sit in your car for just a minute."

"Sit in my car?"

"There's a little matter I need to clear up with you. It won't take long."

"Well, I don't know, I've got to get inside. There's some things I've got—"

I stood between him and the back steps of City Hall.

He knew.

"Like I said, this'll just take a second. You won't miss anything inside."

We got into his car. It wasn't fancy at all. I made it to be around an '86. Cloth seats, a few coins in the ashtray and around the console, takeout napkins on the floor, remnants of a Wendy's soft drink in the cupholder, leftover sections of a newspaper in the back seat. Didn't he ever clean it up?

He wasn't looking at me, but he knew I was taking up a lot of space, even spilling over into his. Things were very tight in this front seat and he twitched in discomfort.

So far, so good.

"I saw Norma last night."

Up went the eyebrows in faked surprise.

"Oh, really? Is she all right? Give her my best, will you?"

"The ride is over, BK."

"Ride? What ride?"

"You know what I mean. From now on, whatever you owe Mambo is *your* problem. She does not give you another nickel. And on top of that, she's not seeing you anymore, either."

At first he wasn't sure what facial expression to wear, whether to keep his wide-eyed "what-do-you-mean" look going or just to admit the whole thing. Embarrassing confessions weren't really in the front of his playbook, though. So for a split second, it looked like he was going to keep up the charade as a natural politician-type reflex.

But then he realized I had him, that I really knew what I was talking about.

He said, "Hey now, whatever she and I want to do is our business, Don Roy. You can't tell me—"

"I can and I am telling you. The ride is over."

"Listen, if she wants to help me out, then she's entitled—"

"I don't think you quite understand me. She doesn't

71

want to. She's back with me now for good, and your little gravy train has reached the end of the line."

Lucky for him I was a lot calmer this morning than I was when Norma laid all this on me last night.

"Who the hell do you think you are, telling me what I can and can't do?"

I'd expected this, the indignation, perfectly timed.

I knew I had to tread very lightly here, yet leave a big footprint. Like I said earlier, this is the mayor, not somebody you can easily shove around.

"BK, I'm just stating a fact, and the fact is that the money lake has dried up. You're gonna have to get it somewhere else."

His lips closed tightly, then through gritted teeth he said, "You know, I could go in there and get your probation officer on the phone. I can get you sent back to prison today for doing this."

Time for the trip out to the end of the limb while BK revs up the chainsaw.

"For doing what? You mean for telling the mayor, who just happens to be a degenerate gambler, that he's gonna have to pay off his own illegal sports bets from now on, that my woman isn't going to do it for him? Like she's been doing for the last three fucking years as a prostitute. And if you bring cops out here to bust me, that's what I'll tell them. And that's what my lawyer will say in open court. That you're using your position to railroad me back inside just because I've upset your sweet little deal involving gambling and prostitution."

There was anger in his eyes, all right, but I could see the fear behind the fire.

Just to make sure he totally understood, I added with a raised eyebrow of my own, "And isn't there an election coming up in the fall? This isn't really the kind of thing that would make you look real good in the eyes of the voters, now, is it?"

He opened the door. As he started to climb out, he turned back to me, saying, "You will live to regret this. You and that cheap fucking slut!"

Instinctively, I wanted to reach over and slap him, but before I could, he was out of the car, so I never made the move. Just as well, because that *could* have violated me back inside.

Probably would have, too.

He walked to the door of City Hall. I didn't follow him.

Instead, I called out, "Remember what I said, BK. The ride is over."

NINE

I needed ID.

Even though I had no plans to leave the island, it was just something I thought I should have. Sort of a knee-jerk reflex kind of thing. I'd always had fake ID for my grifts, for one thing or another, so I kind of felt naked without it.

Yale Lando was the guy in Key West to see for that. Driver's licenses, green cards, birth certificates, college degrees—no job was out of reach for him. He even licensed a few Cuban doctors up in Miami who didn't want the minor inconvenience of having to attend American medical schools.

To top it off, his work was flawless, never questioned. I'd gotten some Nevada ID from him before leaving for Vegas, and I'd referred some others to him over the years.

He worked out of his house on Havana Lane, a

little street tucked away off Truman. The house sat behind a high wooden fence, nearly concealed by a canopy of very big, very old, orange bougainvillea and other heavy vegetation. His equipment was in a mother-in-law apartment in the rear of the house, but I never got to see it.

You always dealt with Yale in his living room, sitting on cheap furniture.

The Price Is Right was on his TV. The host was about to offer a squealing contestant a shot at a new car.

Yale leaned back in his ancient armchair, sipping on a glass of fresh-squeezed grapefruit juice as he ran down my want list and gave me a price. He had to raise his voice a little to be heard over the excitement on the TV.

"Forty-five hundred," he said in his rich Conch accent. "Two grand for the passport, five hundred for the driver's license, and a dime apiece for the two credit cards."

I nodded.

He ran a hand through curly brown hair, then down through a matching beard. I knew we were the same age, but you couldn't tell by looking at his face, so much of it was covered up. His eyes, however, showed the truth, and the backs of his hands had the first faint traces of the gnarl that time would eventually put there.

"Remember, the license and passport will be in the same name, while the credit cards will be in two different names altogether."

"So the passport is backup to the license? In case I'm asked for two forms of ID."

"Check. But the passport will be totally valid for travel out of the country. And the license will be valid also, complete with a backup file in Tallahassee."

I always marveled at Yale's deep connections, how he managed all of this. He moved me over to a makeshift area in his Florida room where he set up a camera on a tripod. I sat down on a small stool as he snapped my photo.

"Light blue," he said, pointing to the backdrop behind me. "That's the color they use on authentic Florida licenses. Any other color and they peg it as a phony. We'll use a white backdrop for the passport."

"Do I pick everything up at the same time?"

"No. On the first deliv — hey, wait a minute!"

His eyes shot back to the TV. The woman contestant said something as he hissed, "No, you stupid bitch! The motor oil is more expensive than the fabric softener!"

He kicked off his sandals and headed back toward the couch, shaking his fist at her.

76

"The motor oil! The motor oil!"

Finally, the woman changed her mind at the last second, selecting the motor oil. It was the right move, so she advanced one step closer to the car.

Relieved, Yale went on. "Anyway, on the first delivery I give you the passport, the license, and one of the two credit cards. You can start using the card right away. It'll have a ten thousand dollar line of credit, and like I said, it'll be in a different name. A totally legit name of a real guy somewhere who actually has his real credit card safely buried in his wallet. This is an exact duplicate, number and all, so the charges will breeze through when you go to make a purchase. The real guy won't ever suspect a thing till he gets his bill."

"So, for all practical purposes, it's a real credit card? Not stolen?"

"Check. Now, you can only use it for a month, of course. Visa sends out their bills on the twenty-third of each month. So you can use this card until about the twenty-fifth of April. That's when the real guy'll get his bill, around that time, and naturally the shit will hit the fan when he sees what's happened. Then, on that date, you just cut up that card and come back here. I'll give you another card in another name. Also good for ten dimes. That'll see you through till May twenty-fifth. Okay?"

77

"Okay."

"Now, you can buy stuff around town with these cards, but just a little, not too much, all right? You don't want a lot of charges showing up from here. It's too small a town and too easy for the feds to cover. Remember, this's a federal offense."

He looked me straight in the eye, letting that one sink in. His eyes were the color of a summer sky, so bright I almost wanted to smile. But I pushed back the urge.

Then he said, "So if you really want to go to town, make some big buys, run up to Miami and do it. They'll never be able to track you up there. Except don't buy anything that's traceable in itself, like a car."

I agreed that was the way to go, so that seemed to close out our business. He got up to refill his grapefruit juice.

When he came back from the kitchen he turned his attention back to his TV. The woman was guessing prices or something, I don't know, while the host was becoming more breathless the closer she got to winning the car. The audience was getting more and more worked up as well. Yale seemed to be really into it.

"You know," he said, "this is truly the greatest show ever to be on TV."

He turned thoughtful here, kind of like a bearded

philosopher, who was used to having his every word absorbed by anxious students sitting at his feet.

"They've managed to boil down the entire human experience to a few minutes of greed. Ordinary people, people like you and I know, like we grew up with, behaving like mad dogs for the chance to win a 'fortune in *fabulous prizes!*'" He said it just like those overheated TV announcers. "When those jerks get up on stage with Bob Barker, they have only one purpose in their miserable lives. To grab as much swag as they can, as quick as they can. And to do it in front of the whole country while drooling all over themselves."

I remembered this show. It had been on forever. Like an old friend who came to dinner and never left.

"They go crazy when they win this shit, right?"

"Check. It's like it validates their entire existence. You know, like their lives have meant something after all. They've been to the mountaintop with Bob Barker."

As soon as he said that, the woman won the car and went apeshit.

"Look," Yale said. "What'd I tell you? And if she'd lost, you can bet she'd go the rest of her life feeling like a complete failure. Forty years from now, she'd be telling her friends at the nursing home, 'You know, if only I'd guessed a higher price for that motor oil, I'd've won the damn car'." He chuckled out loud. "I guarantee you, bubba, every one of these people would buy one of those credit cards from me if they had the chance. Every fucking one of them."

"You think so?"

"I know so. They all want the new car, the free lunch, and they don't mind tippy-toeing a little on the other side of the line to get it. Especially if you can make them believe they'll never get caught."

"When can I get the goods?"

I didn't really want to get Yale off the subject. I could tell he was getting fairly intense here, making a pretty provocative point, but I had to get going.

"Try me...in about two weeks, okay?"

"Okay, but today's the twenty-ninth. Two weeks, that'll be around April twelfth. That's only going to give me just a little less than two weeks on the first credit card."

He looked away from the TV. They'd gone to a commercial. But he didn't look at me.

"Don Roy, you know when I give you a figure, that's it. You don't jew me down."

He paused for just a moment. I didn't say anything. I figured he was still working the count. Then he eyed me.

"But because we were altar boys together, and because we sat next to each other in English class two years in a row, I'm gonna drop three hundred from my original quote. Besides, you're right. It wouldn't be fair, because you're only getting two weeks play on the card." He thought for a second, then he said, "But I'll need half now, the other half on delivery."

I gave him twenty-one hundred dollars as we shook hands.

I was about to leave when he said, "Hey man, don't go now. You gotta stick around. The Showcase Showdown's coming up. It's the best part."

I thanked him again and left.

TEN

I woke up next to Norma for the first time in nearly seven years. I had a hard time believing my good fortune.

Here I was, home only three days, but already I had a few grand in my pocket, another two hundred large on its way, a deal working for permanent ID, and the woman of my dreams peacefully sleeping next to me. Well, okay, maybe she wasn't exactly the woman of my dreams, you know, like Raquel Welch or somebody, but she was plenty good enough for me.

A lot more than I ever thought I could get.

You see, I was never what you'd call a real attractive guy to begin with, being so big and bullnecked, you know what I mean? I just looked like a big old galoot with big arms, big hands, and an intimidating appearance.

Not the kind of guy that the foxy girls are drawn

to.

Never the slim, honey-voiced guy with the right clothes or the slick red car, bringing his model-gorgeous girl to a trendy nightclub.

Rather, I was always the anonymous, faceless bouncer type, working the door, pulling back the velvet rope for them to pass through, saying "Welcome."

The thing is, I'm probably a lot smarter than most of those red convertible-type guys. I'm really good with numbers—I've always been able to do quick calculations and figure odds.

And I can spot character flaws in people immediately.

Weeding out the bullshit artists from the heavy hitters is no problem for me. I can practically do it blind.

But no girl ever gave me a chance in high school.

Afterward, though, I got a few chances, but I usually blew them sky-high. I would never know the right things to say to a girl, you know, like in conversation when you're just getting to know them. It never came easy for me. Other guys always seemed to have the words I wished I could say.

I know I must've seemed like some pathetic baboon way out of his element. Not only that, my brainpower, along with the rest of the real me, had a hard time showing itself.

Money was never a problem, though. I always had plenty of it to spend, so spend it I did. That's where a lot of the dough I made from my early scores went, on these girls I kept trying to impress.

That's how it went, year in and year out, just one piece of bad news after another.

Until Norma.

I found her serving drinks one night at this little locals' spot over in one of the neighborhoods. Her second husband had just dumped her, so she was definitely rebounding.

She wasn't what you'd call a knockout. Hell, I guess you could say she wasn't even that good-looking, but once I got to know her a little, I could see her insides. You know, they glowed like a warm summer sunset, while her smile was just the biggest and brightest thing I'd ever seen. Whenever she turned it toward me, it damn sure made everything right again.

She evidently found something in me that she thought was worthwhile, because once we linked up—I guess it was back around eighty-two or three—we were solid, I mean tighter than three coats of paint.

Even now, I can hear her whispering, "Don Roy, I'll make you so proud of me."

You have no idea what that meant to me, hearing

her say something like that. No one, but no one, had ever felt that way toward me before. Or since.

So I hope you can see how I was so quick to forgive her for what she did while I was gone. Hell, there's times when we've all got to do things we don't want to do—God knows I've done a few pretty disgusting things that I thought were necessary at the time.

Norma was always a real confused girl. I guess she figured she was only trying to get by when she left me for that fucking weasel BK just before I split for Vegas. He was right when he said I couldn't afford to take her with me. That's when he apparently made his move on her, so she took the bait.

You've got to understand something. See, to a girl like Norma, having someone like BK come sniffing around you is a big deal, because that kind of guy is usually way, way out of reach. The fact that he was married wasn't important.

He's from one of the oldest families on the island, with plenty of dough, and his life damn well set up. But there he was, making like he cared for her. That was the play. She had nothing better going for her. I was leaving soon for Vegas.

What was the point of refusing?

***

Norma had just dropped me off at Mambo's later in the day when I saw the car out of the side of my eye.

A big silver Mercedes, out of place in this neighborhood, sat on the corner. As soon as Norma pulled away, it hummed to life, then rolled up alongside me. The front seat passenger door opened as a guy about my size stepped out. He had long blonde hair, down around his shoulders. I didn't know him.

"Get in the car," he said, in an accent that wasn't from around here.

He opened the back door, pointing my way inside. He obviously didn't know me, either, or else he wouldn't have ordered me around that way.

"Ask me nice and I'll just walk away without telling you to go fuck yourself."

"Mr Whitney would like to see you."

His tone was still flat, without feeling. His broad shoulders and thick biceps bulged under a tight black T-shirt. He was no stranger to the gym. Confidence spread all over his youngish face.

"Whitney? Which one? BK or the old man?"

"Former mayor Wilson Whitney Senior," he said, now with a little zing in his voice.

Punks like him are always trying to impress you with who they know.

"Is this how he makes his appointments? Snatching people off the street?"

His buddy got out of the driver's side. He was also about my size and he had long hair, too, only it was dark brown. He didn't move, though, he just stood there glaring at me.

I guess he thought I'd jump right in after seeing the two of them.

"What's he want with me? I don't even know him."

I knew I would go, even if it was just out of curiosity, but I wasn't going to make it easy for them.

"Just get in the car, Doyle," the driver said.

Everything about him told me he was the ringleader of this little duo, so I looked over the roof of the car at him.

"Not till I know what this's all about. Otherwise, you can kiss my ass."

Tight T-shirt developed a little tic under his left eye. His sidekick's jaw tightened beneath a reddening face.

I knew the rough stuff was only moments away.

"Get in the fucking car, asshole!" said the T-shirt.

He grabbed my arm, jostling me toward the gaping rear door.

"Milton, *no!*" cried the driver.

Too late. I'd wheeled around behind Milton,

87

pulling his arm into a hammerlock, while grabbing a handful of his long blonde hair. I slammed his head into the frame of the big car, where the roof meets the front door. He fell to the sidewalk, bleeding from the gash on his forehead.

The driver rushed around to his fallen comrade, putting a handkerchief over the wound.

While he knelt over Milton, I said before sliding into the back seat, "Now let's go see your boss, and you can explain how Milton's blood spilled all over these nice leather seats."

SETUP ON FRONT STREET

ELEVEN

Wilson Whitney lived out in Key Haven, the closest thing there is to a suburb around here. It's actually on Stock Island, the first island up from Key West.

Living up there gives you a lot more space than you can get in town, and of course the taxes are a whole lot less because it's outside the city limits. Before moving up there, he occupied a huge family home on William Street right in the middle of town, but instead of selling it, he gave it to BK and Rita somewhere along the line.

I guess he was afraid his ancestors would put a curse on him if he ever sold the house to a non-Whitney.

After a brief stop at the hospital to drop Milton off at the emergency room, we pulled into the driveway of the big man's house. Up on the veranda, the driver opened the big double doors to the house, motioning for me to go in.

The place was relatively new—what I mean is, it wasn't as old as a lot of the houses back in town.

The way it looked when you walked in, I mean, you just knew that someone with major bucks lived there. Gleaming tile floors gave the whole place a wide-open, Mexican look, and fancy lighting fixtures stuck out from every corner. Sunlight rushed in through big front windows and adjoining open rooms, making everything look airy and inviting.

As I walked through the foyer, I caught the smell of some heavy meat dish simmering back in the kitchen. A uniformed Cuban maid dusted a big, black grand piano in the living room. She was pretty in the way that only Latin women can be.

I wondered if she thought this was the best she could do in life.

The driver led me into a dim study where the old man sat, shuffling papers around on his desk. Thick green curtains covered the windows, allowing only a sliver or two of sunlight to peek in.

A floor lamp provided some light. It wasn't enough.

A big, matching leather couch and chair set took up one corner of the room. Behind the desk a floor-to-ceiling bookcase stretched across the wall, filled with

---

leather-bound books in sets, where they all looked alike. The other walls had lots of plaques and shit, just like with Sully.

What's the deal here? Once you get a little respect, you're supposed to plaster it all over your walls?

"Thank you, Bradley," he said.

The driver left the room, shutting the door.

"Please sit down, Don Roy."

Without offering a handshake, he pointed toward one of two comfortable-looking leather chairs opposite the big desk. I sat in the other one.

"My son tells me you and he were in high school together, is that right?"

He appeared to be pushing seventy, but looked a long way from frail. He was not the least bit overweight, and his posture was erect. His eyes were vigilant, overcast-gray, like his full head of hair, while his voice brimmed with strength and authority.

"That's right. We graduated the same year."

"I thought I knew everyone in his class, but I don't remember you."

"You wouldn't. I didn't make much of a splash."

But *he* had a big presence, I had to admit.

He was one of these guys who was used to having power and plenty of it. Kind of a natural-born top dog. He generally got his way with everyone he came in

---

91

contact with.

Especially the lower species like myself.

"Well, be that as it may...I'll come right to the point."

He shifted in his chair a little more toward me. I caught it.

"You are not to interfere with my son's gambling or with the manner in which he pays his debts. Do you understand?"

"Provided your son doesn't expect my woman to prostitute herself for the sole purpose of giving him the money."

His voice softened. "Don Roy, look. My son likes to gamble. Maybe a little too much, I'll admit, and maybe I've been too lenient with him. But from what I understand, they're seeing each other...they've been friends for quite a while...so let's just let it go for now.

"It's like I told BK this morning, Mr Whitney, I'm taking Norma out of that place, and she's through paying his debts."

His teeth clenched just a little while his head moved forward, but he was trying to keep his voice at an easygoing level. He wasn't succeeding.

"I know you just got back home after being away for several years," he said. "Things change when you stay gone like that. Sometimes the change isn't to your liking."

He leaned back a little in his expensive chair and relaxed his shoulders, his fingers interlaced in front of him on his stomach.

"Let's look at this the way it really is," he went on. "I know my son fooled around with her for awhile before all this...before she...started helping him out. He showed her a good time for a couple of years and...well, now she's just paying him back, is all."

I could tell he liked that one. The smug SOB. That really made sense to him.

Norma was just repaying BK for all the wonderful things he did for her. Like honoring her with his dick in her mouth whenever he could slip away from his wife.

Yes sir, now there's one she owes him.

What is it with these people?

Then he leaned all the way back in his chair and spread his hands out in front of him.

"Besides, this is the nineties. We've got to be broadminded about this sort of thing."

I gripped the arms of the chair and clenched my teeth. Then I reached down into the front pocket of my guayabera for the red dice and began silently grinding them inside my big fist.

After a moment of this, I could speak.

My voice was ice. "BK's free ride is over. And that's

final."

"From what I understand, this bookie is very impatient with people who owe him money. If it were anyone else, I'd deal directly with him, but he's a DeLima. His family and mine have had sort of an understanding over the years, so I don't question his policies. If he says my son has to pay up, then that's the way it is. So we move down a couple of levels, and that's where we find you and your...girlfriend."

He was looking so far down his nose at me, I felt like I was in another area code.

"Move to whatever level you want, but the elevator doesn't stop at Norma's floor."

His upper body then moved as far forward as possible without leaving his chair.

"All right, I'll lay it out for you. I don't really care about his gambling. I don't even care about the money. And I certainly don't give a damn about this slimy Stock Island whore in that back-alley brothel. But when you blow back into town, fresh out of prison, and start pushing my son around, my son the *mayor*, I might add, then you've got trouble. So your price for avoiding that trouble is to stay out of my son's private life."

I ground the dice together harder and harder.

"I didn't push anybody —"

"Shut up!"

He put his palms down on the desk and almost stood up.

"Who the hell do you think you're talking to, you fucking ape! My family's been on this island seven generations, and you come in here telling *me* what my son is going to do with some whore who fucks niggers and Cubans all night long? If he wants to ship her up to Miami to work the *streets*, he'll do it! Without any shit from you!" Then he sat back and added, "Unless that girl resumes her duties, this might be the most expensive conversation you've ever had."

He was pissing me off, but that was about it. I was getting ready for the "you're-going-back-to-prison" speech.

My eyebrows raised, then my head tilted a little, asking him silently what he meant, thinking I knew the answer.

He said, "Yes, I said expensive. I know you're back here looking for the money that Irish saloonkeeper is holding back from you. You lay off my son or you'll never get it."

Whoa, where'd this come from? Now it was my turn to lean forward.

I said, "You're the one who's — "

"Don't bother with a comment. Today is Friday. If the girl's not back to work by tomorrow night, you'll never see the money. And I'll know if she's there, because I own the building. *Bradley!*"

The door flew open and Bradley appeared.

"Take him back to town."

SETUP ON FRONT STREET

TWELVE

By Sunday night I'd moved out of the rooming house and in with Norma.

Her apartment was pretty nice, with a sweeping view of the parking lot, but with the two of us in there, it was small. No room for anything. That's what she kept saying, anyway.

I told her if she'd spent three years in a tiny cell with a jigaboo gangbanger, she'd think this place was the fucking penthouse suite at Caesars Palace.

We'd ordered out for pizza. The room was dark except for some sitcom she had on the TV, along with whatever light drifted in from the kitchen. The air conditioning cooled things off nicely. Norma felt good curled up next to me on the couch.

"So what're you gonna do now?" she asked.

"Well, first thing is, I'm gonna have a beer before the pizza gets here."

She playfully slapped my arm.

"No-o-oo. You know what I mean. What're you gonna do from now on?"

I pushed the remote button to lower the TV volume.

"Like I told you, tomorrow I come into some money. It'll be a lot, and it can hold us for a good while, but not forever. We *will* have time to plan things out, though."

I held her closer to me, then lowered my voice accordingly. "Think about it, honey. It's gonna be a little easier. No more pressures of having to make the rent. Or a car payment. We can have a few nice things. A little breathing room for a change. And now that you're out of the Fun House, there'll be no going back. How do you like that?"

"Oh, it sounds wonderful. Just wonderful. I hope we can 'plan things', as you say, so that we won't have to go back to the way things used to be."

She turned her head up from my chest so she could look at me.

"You know, a couple of months ago, there was this guy on Oprah who said planning a better life is something everybody ought to sit down and do. Like, he said you should sit down with a pencil and paper and actually make a list of things in life you want to do.

But he said that sticking with that plan is really, really hard, and that most people fail. We won't fail, will we, Don Roy?"

Before I could tell her no, she sighed, "You know, all I want...I just want us to have a...a...future."

That was a word she'd always had trouble with. The concept was pretty hard for her to comprehend.

Fact is, I'd never really had a solid grip on it myself.

I'd always lived in the weedy undergrowth of straight society, raised in one of those dried-out-white shotgun houses on the edge of Old Town, scraping through on a mix of wits and muscle. My adult life was a blur of moving from score to score, then back into the safety of the shadows.

I usually got by all right, but how could I, or Norma for that matter, see our "future" the way everyone else saw theirs? Our futures growled in front of us, like a dark, curvy, mountain road full of big potholes and upturned nails.

Small wonder, with the way we were brought up, the way we steered our lives. Very few doors were ever open for us, so we took what limited choices we had.

Shit, who could blame us?

THIRTEEN

It was barely dawn Monday morning when the repeated pounding on the door woke me up. Not with knuckles, but with a fist.

The sound was unmistakable.

Cops.

Norma threw on a robe. She stood at the door yelling, "Who is it?"

"Police! Open up."

As she opened the door, I already had my pants on. I heard his distinct Cuban-Conch accent.

"Where is he? Where's Doyle?"

Ortega.

He shoved his way into the apartment, followed by his plain-clothes partner and two uniforms. Norma's objections trailed off into space.

I moved out into the living room. As he approached me, the only thing between us was his attitude. It was way out in front of him, like cheap cologne.

"Looks like you fucked up big-time, Doyle."

His sneer really got to me. I wanted to slice it right off his wise-ass face.

"Today's April Fool's Day, Ortega. This your idea of a joke?"

"The joke's on you, big man. But you probably won't think it's too funny."

I could tell by his smirk he thought it was hilarious.

"Okay, it's tearing me up. Now, what's your beef? And make it snappy. I want to go back to bed."

"You might be sleeping in county facilities by nightfall. Where were you last night?"

"Right here. What's the deal?"

"Can you prove it?"

His eyes wandered downward to my bare shoulders and chest, checking out my jailhouse tats.

"Yeah. Norma here was with me the whole—"

"Oh, right! This bitch. Like she's a real reliable fucking witness."

"Witness? To what? What's this all about?"

The uniforms had unhooked their clubs from their belts. They were slapping them into their palms, almost in sync with one another. Warning me not to get out of line, yet itching for me to do just that.

He got right up in my face, I mean real close. This was the first time anyone had done that in years and not been knocked flat on his ass.

"Your fucking pal Frankie Sullivan is what this is all about. It seems he went and got his throat slit last night. We found him down on Front Street, face down in the gutter."

He backed off an inch or two, then added, "Funny, I thought you Irish assholes had some kind of secret agreement between you, you know, like, not to kill each other."

Norma shrieked. As for me, my shoulders sagged, while my knees went limp. I almost fell back on the chair behind me.

"Sully...he's *dead?* You telling me he's *dead?*"

Ortega turned to his pals and said, "Don't they have some kind of agreement? Where they swear on St Patrick or something?"

They all nodded and smiled at that one.

Then he said, "Look at the fake surprise!" He strutted around the room, mocking my raspy voice. "'He's dead? I didn't know he was dead!' Like you were some kind of innocent fucking citizen. Like you were at a church bake sale while Sullivan was getting his neck torn open."

The other cops chuckled at his performance. The

jerkoff should be on the stage somewhere. Anywhere but here.

He put his own face back on as he turned back to me.

"All right, Doyle, how do you want to do this? The easy way or the hard way?"

Words choked in the back of my throat. "I...I swear, Ortega, I...I didn't know anything about this. Sully was—"

"Yeah, I know, he was your closest fucking friend. I hope you reminded him of that while you were turning out his lights." He pointed toward Norma. "Now you say you were laying up in her titties all last night. But you're gonna need a better alibi than that, my man. Much better."

"Ortega, I swear to you, I didn't do it. I had no reason to--"

"Oh, you had reason, all right. He was holding your cut of that diamond job the two of you pulled three years ago. And his wife claims you threatened him with bodily harm if he didn't fork it over. Right there's aggravated assault. A felony in itself. Then, we find him lying in a puddle of blood with a big smile on his neck. And you with an alibi that won't hold up."

He stepped back smiling, satisfied with his own read on this whole thing.

Then he said, "Now how's that for a motive? And what do you think your future looks like now?"

"Look, Ortega, if it happened late at night on Front Street, for Chrissakes, it could've been —"

"Some street punk? Sticking him up for the cash in his pocket?"

"Yeah. Why not?"

He shook his head. "Uh-uh. His money was still on him. Nearly seven hundred clams. And he had no reason to be down there at one-thirty this morning. That was the time of death. He lives — or should I say lived--up on Petronia Street off Georgia. As you leave his bar, I'm sure you know that's in the exact opposite direction from Front Street. And I'm told he always went straight home every night. Unless he stopped off for some pussy from one of his girlfriends. And I doubt any of them live down there."

His partner helped himself to a seat on the couch. Ortega waited for my response to his neatly wrapped-up spin on the whole thing.

I guess he thought I'd just break down and spit it all out for him. You know, how I dragged or suckered Sully into a car and drove him to the other side of downtown, where I knifed him in a fit of rage over the money, then dumped him on the street.

Shows you how this cop thinks.

Like a fucking amateur.

"That's pretty amazing police work," I said right back at him. "Dick Tracy would be proud of you. Or did you get that from reading Sherlock Holmes?"

He turned around to face his club-swinging goons.

Gesturing back toward me, he said, "We got a big man here, boys. Thinks he's the biggest fucking man in the Keys. Truth is, he's just another overgrown punk who thinks he's hot shit."

They nodded on cue, slapping their sticks a little harder into their palms.

For effect, of course.

"You really think I did this?" I asked him.

Of course the answer was yes, and naturally, I knew who really did do it. Or who had ordered it, anyway.

"You ever know Sullivan to go down there after hours?" he asked me. "Was he really that stupid? Or maybe he liked to go down there trolling for whores and coke dealers?"

"Ask yourself this, Ortega. Am I really that stupid? To threaten him, then put him down, and *then* leave him out in the street? It's a fucking wonder you didn't find a bloody knife right there with my initials on it. Or maybe you think it's still in my pants pocket."

"Oh, you're that stupid, all right. Besides, no one

else could've done it. Sullivan was well-liked all over town. No one else had a motive."

The thing was, I couldn't tell this idiot who really did it.

Number one, he'd never believe me.

Number two, he didn't have the balls to go after someone of Whitney's caliber.

The old man was loaded with power in this town, and few had what it took to go up against him. Me, I was an easy target. I had a motive for sure: Sully owed me the money, so I did threaten him. He probably told his wife about it Wednesday night when he got home, then she spilled it to Ortega after getting the bad news this morning.

Bringing Whitney's name up right now was useless.

And accusing him of murder? Killing some nightclub owner that he had no connection to? Forget it.

I had no response.

Ortega had one.

"Get dressed," he said. "We're going downtown."

FOURTEEN

The session downtown lasted about an hour and a half. It consisted mostly of Ortega talking tough, while practicing interrogation-room tactics he'd seen on *Kojak* reruns.

I ran over my story a hundred times, denying, of course, that I ever threatened Sully or even leaned on him for money. For that matter, I claimed that the diamond job was a frame to begin with, so therefore, there *was* no money.

Even though I couldn't prove I was asleep at the time of the hit, they didn't have any hard evidence to hold me on. The pizza delivery boy could put me at Norma's around nine, and no one could put me on Front Street at one-thirty.

As I walked out of the station, though, I knew this scene would be repeated in living color whenever they picked up the slightest lead that they could connect to me.

***

Norma went to visit her mother around noon up on Big Coppitt Key, about ten miles up the road, so she dropped me off downtown before she left. I hoofed it down to the South Beach Restaurant for lunch.

It was a nifty little sandblown place right on the water, over on the Atlantic side, but still kind of out of the way. I was glad it was still there.

I took a table on the edge of the outdoor seating area, right off the beach itself. It felt terrific to be sitting there in the ocean breeze, soaking up the open sunshine.

A complete one-eighty from prison.

There's nothing colder than prison concrete. The dark desolation...the tense friction. Hardened men scraping up against each other all the time, the constant looking over your shoulder year in and year out—it all messes with your mind, you know?

Makes you think sometimes that you're no better than any of those fucking animals in there. I don't even like thinking about it.

But now, finally, I was through with it.

Human again.

SETUP ON FRONT STREET

I removed my sunglasses to look directly out at the wide, sparkling waters of the Florida Straits. Gazing out toward Cuba, my thoughts went back to my boyhood.

Back then, the tourists hadn't yet invaded us in such big numbers, so we were pretty much all by ourselves down here. I could still taste the salt on my tongue from swimming off Higgs Beach every morning of the long, tropical summers, as well as every afternoon during the school year. Then, after shaking off the sand, I'd run to play baseball.

What I'm trying to say is that I was a pretty normal kid. Back then, the conniver that I would become was still forming deep down inside me. All the brainwork and the hustles that would surface later on were dormant, but every so often, I could feel them trying to push their way out. Even then, I was aware of the angles, trying to twist everything to my advantage, doing whatever it took to get me one up.

But for those few short years before the real world would come to claim me, I just wanted to enjoy what little innocence I had. Could you blame me? I really, really thought that was how it would always be, all swimming and baseball. Never imagining the cruel surprises life had in store.

Shows you what I knew.

The cooked vegetables on my plate had all my attention when she came up to my table.

"Hello, Don Roy."

Her familiar, deep voice hit me hard. I put my fork down and looked up.

"Rita? Is that you?"

I had to look again. She leaned on the rail next to my table. The voice was hers, but it came out of a brand new look.

Twenty or thirty pounds had disappeared, while her long, stringy hair that I remembered had been chopped off and permed. Its dishwater brown color had turned blonde somewhere along the way, warming up the icy blue in her eyes. Her sensible white cotton dress clung to her new curves for dear life, allowing a trace of cleavage to peek through. I noticed beads of sweat on her neck and upper chest. She'd been walking in the heat. Her open shoes showed cherry red toenails that matched her manicured fingernails and lipstick. Long, slender fingers slid a slim cigarette out of its package.

As she stoked it up, I began to sweat a little myself.

What had BK done to deserve a wife like this?

"Yep. Nobody but me," she replied. "Mind if I sit down?"

I motioned toward the other white plastic chair at

my table.

"Help yourself."

She spoke just above whisper level, even though there was no one around to hear us. "God, it wasn't this hot when I left the house this morning. It's like the sun just went into overdrive all of a sudden."

It was hot, all right, and getting hotter around this table.

"Want something to drink?"

"Actually, I'd love an iced tea."

I thought I saw her squinting behind her designer sunglasses. I signaled the waitress with the order.

Meanwhile, I couldn't take my eyes off her. A couple of tiny little diamonds perked up her pierced ears and a tasteful thin gold bracelet wrapped her wrist. A pretty good-sized diamond perched up high off her ring finger.

But she didn't really need jewelry.

She looked good all by herself.

I blurted it out. "You're sure looking good."

She smiled, then looked down. I saw the beginnings of a blush. Then she reined it back in.

"I've tried to slim down a little."

She eyed me directly again as she spread her arms out a little bit, showing herself off. Ta-da!

"What do you think of the new me?"

"I think BK is the luckiest guy in town. You really look great!"

She aimed a big smile at me, lots of pretty white teeth. Straight, too.

"Well, thank *you*, sir. But it's really been hard work, shedding those pounds." She then went into the story of her makeover. I nodded in all the right places.

The waitress brought the tea. Rita immediately sipped from it, then exhaled hard, while she held the cold glass to her neck and throat. Her exhale slid into a low moan, as the glass cooled her off.

Right then, I remembered my mother doing the same thing before we got our air conditioner.

It was back when I was still in grade school.

That summer was particularly hot—though the heat never used to bother me nearly as much as it did her.

One of her boyfriends—I forget which one, but it was one of the ones that lived with us for awhile—told her to get him a beer. Pretty soon she came back from the kitchen with a beer in one hand and a glass of iced tea in the other. He guzzled the beer, then burped loud and long.

But I could see my mother now, as vividly as I just saw Rita, hold that cold glass to her throat, then moan with pleasure. She did it a lot, I guess, but that was the one specific time I clearly remember.

Also, she was wearing some kind of white clingy thing like Rita had on now. It might've been just a slip or a nightgown rather than a dress, but it gave off a similar look.

On Rita, however, the whole thing was arousing.

I wasn't ten years old anymore.

While I was trapped in this memory for quite a few seconds, I glimpsed the beach.

No one seemed to be moving much. Small waves lapped gently at the shore and the light breeze tried hard to cool things down. Someone's radio played *Like A Virgin*.

"Did you know I was in this little out-of-the-way spot?" I finally asked. "Or did you just happen to walk all the way down here?"

I glanced around the place. Not many customers. They appeared to be mostly tourists, a couple of spring breaker types, along with a foreigner or two, right off the beach, most of them still in swimsuits. No locals.

She smirked a little as she drank some more iced tea.

"I was in the pharmacy up on the corner and I saw you walk by. I heard you were back in town. How's it going?"

What a question. "Well, I was doing okay until

early this morning. Someone killed Frankie Sullivan last night and they think I did it."

It happened too late at night to make the morning paper, so I wondered if she knew about it.

She showed no surprise as she drew deep on her long, thin cigarette. The breeze from the ocean blew away the smoke but not the heat.

"Well, did you do it?" she asked.

She took off her shades, penetrating my eyes with hers.

"You know I didn't. I wouldn't."

That was all I wanted to say on the subject. But she had a little more to add.

"It was all because of BK and his gambling, wasn't it."

The way she put it, it wasn't really a question.

I took a sip of my own iced tea. It needed more lemon.

"What's the deal, Rita? What do you know about all this? And why are you here?"

I squeezed the last of the lemon juice into the tea.

She crushed out her cigarette. "I never knew you too well, Don Roy," she said, as if she were letting me in on a big secret, "but I knew who you were. I knew a little about you."

She reached into her purse for her cigarettes.

Pulling them out, she shook another one out of the package.

"Even though you were a couple of years ahead of me in high school, I'd heard about you, and like I said, I knew who you were. I knew that in school you were always into gambling and things like that. Then after I graduated, and for years afterward, I'd see you around town from time to time and you never seemed to be working. You know, you were always walking around in the middle of the day...that kind of thing."

I was more than a little surprised that she'd been keeping this kind of watch on me for so long. Flame leaped from her gold lighter, firing up her cigarette and throwing a yellow glow onto her face, while her lively eyes bored into mine. The way she did it, it was straight out of a movie. Lauren Bacall zapping Bogie with those come-on eyes from behind a lit cigarette.

Making his dick hard.

"You ever have a regular job?" she asked.

"Rita, what's this all about?"

"Just tell me, did you ever have a regular job?"

"Well...not really."

"Why not? I want to know why you never went out and looked for a job. Just like everyone else."

"What are you, writing my life story here?"

"Just answer me. Why didn't you get a job?"

MIKE DENNIS

"Why do you want to —"

"Just...answer...the question."

I caved. "Because it was easier not to."

I felt like the final witness on *Perry Mason*, blurting out my confession just so she would quit badgering me.

"Easier not to? Why was it easier?"

"Rita, what's —"

"Just why was it easier?"

"Why do you want to know?"

"Just answer me, for Chrissakes!"

"Because...well...because there's me, and then there's all of them."

Finally, she leaned back in her chair, then crossed her legs, satisfied she'd gotten the answer she wanted.

"You mean you never really felt like you were a part of regular society here, right? You felt you had no real shot by jumping in the water and rolling along with the prevailing tide, swimming around with everybody else. Being employed was part of that scene, and since you wanted no part of it, you had to get by some other way. Am I right?"

In a way, I was really put off by all of this shit — this was none of her business — but in another way, it twisted my head around.

And it tweaked my curious bone like only raw truth can.

SETUP ON FRONT STREET

The way she put it, it was, well, right on the money. Like she really understood. Besides, I was caught up in all her intensity, especially when it broke through in that deep, sexy voice of hers.

"Yeah, you're right," I replied.

"Well, you want to know something? I felt the same way. Oh, I never gambled or anything like that, but I moved here with my parents when I was thirteen. My father was career Navy, and he eventually retired down here. So we stayed."

She paused for a little effect, downing the last of her iced tea.

"And because I wasn't a Conch—you know, born here—I was always on the outside of things in high school. You know how that goes. But one day, I met BK and I did what it took to win him over. I mean, *whatever* it took."

I caught the drift.

She looked away from me, out toward the ocean. A gigantic cruise ship had appeared on the distant horizon, fresh out of some Caribbean port. Gazing absently at the ship, she twirled a few short strands of hair near the back of her neck.

She said without thinking, "There were a lot of Conch girls after him, you know."

"Well, you must've done something right, because

you've been together for a lot of years now."

She waved that off as her eyes returned to mine. Her voice modulated downward to hiss level.

"Together, shit! You think I'm Barbra Streisand, all googoo-eyed over Robert Redford? You think we're living happily ever after in some fairy tale? What else could I look forward to in this town? What was I going to do, marry a lineman for City Electric? And go to my grave worrying about rent? Shi-it. Not this daddy's girl."

The waitress refilled Rita's tea from a pitcher. She took a long, cold pull from it. It looked like it chased away some of the heat.

Then she said, "Like you, I knew there was no sense in walking when I could ride."

Suddenly, my shoulders relaxed. I felt comfortable talking with her, like we were both listening to the same radio station.

"So you hooked onto BK's bumper and let him do the driving."

"Right. And now, after eighteen years, I've got him covered like a tent."

"So why're you telling me all this?"

She took a deep drag on her cigarette, then slowly let the smoke out in a thin, gray trail. The breeze took it away again.

118

"Because I don't want to see you get framed for this Sullivan killing."

"But why should you care? I mean, you and I never —"

"It's not about you and me," she said quietly. "It's the old man."

She knew. She knew the whole damn story. But I had to speak carefully here. Very carefully.

"You mean Mr Whitney? What about him?"

"I mean it's time that old bastard got what's coming to him."

True, but I wasn't about to jump into that swamp just yet. I needed a little more commitment from her.

"Wait a minute. He's your father-in-law. A lot of people around here think he's tops. He's been a —"

"He's a piece of shit!" She spit that sentence out.

"Keep going."

"He did everything he could to keep BK from marrying me. He treated me like shit! Like I was some kind of worthless bimbo that wasn't nearly good enough for his fucking boy-king son. Do you know that he even tried to buy me off?"

I didn't know about any of this. My face said as much.

"That's right. He offered me five thousand dollars to leave town and forget I ever knew BK. I mean, five thousand fucking dollars! The cheap son of a bitch! Like he didn't want to turn loose of any more to save his precious fucking son! Like I'm some kind of a grade Z slut!"

She took a couple of rapid puffs on her cigarette and calmed her voice down a notch. "Not that I would've taken ten thousand, you understand, or even fifteen. It's just the idea that he not only thought he could buy me out of BK's life, but that he figured my price was so fucking low."

I looked straight at her. Like everyone, she had a price. Hers was obviously higher than the five dimes Whitney was willing to shell out way back when. But not so high that she would turn down the easy life that BK could give her.

Her upper lip curled into a sneer. "So I want that old buzzard to get what's coming to him. And to get it in spades."

She washed that down with some tea. An ice cube landed in her mouth, so she chewed on it for a second, then mumbled around it, "He shouldn't've underestimated me."

My turn to speak. "The cops'll never believe he had anything to do with Sully's killing. And I'm sure he's got an ironclad alibi."

"You bet your ass he does. He was out with BK and

me last night. Him and his new fucking girlfriend. We had a late dinner, then over to the Casa Marina for drinks, and then we all went out to his house, and he made sure we stayed there till after two. He and the girl went up to bed and BK and I left and went home."

"Well, of course he wouldn't've hit Sully himself, anyway."

"It was probably those two goons of his. Milton and Bradley."

"Maybe, but I doubt it. They're too close to him. More than likely, he gave the order to one of them—probably Bradley. Then Bradley farmed it out to someone else. That way no one but Bradley can connect the killing to the old man."

"And if he does, he cooks his own goose."

"Right."

She stubbed out her cigarette as she got up from the table, making a minor adjustment on her hair.

"Listen, Don Roy, if there's anything I can do to help you out of this jam, you let me know. Here's my number—my private number at home."

A pen appeared from her purse as she jotted down the number and slid it across the table at me. Reaching toward my face, she brushed my cheek, her fierce red nails lightly scratching me.

Her smile was wicked, full of everything that a

woman was all about.

She said, "Remember, I said *anything*."

FIFTEEN

Shimmy sat across from me in the dim corner booth at Mambo's.

Last time I saw him, he was a fresh-faced kid, a wheel man making pickups for Mambo's bolita operation. He'd lost a lot of his boyish look since then, even though he was still somewhere in his twenties. He was a tough kid and pretty well-built, not afraid to mix it up if he had to.

Now he was running a high-stakes poker game out of one of the big resort hotels here in town. Normally, these places frown on that kind of thing, but the hotel's GM was a big player himself, so he was only too happy to set aside one of his rooms for the game.

It was a once-a-week thing, so Shimmy brought some of the high-limit players down from Miami and Fort Lauderdale, plus any of the rich hotel guests who could be lured into the game by well-paid concierges.

123

He told me they played at the $100-$200 level with a high rake, which meant that he was pulling in, after expenses and before Mambo's cut, about three dimes a week.

The waiter brought us a couple of beers. Shimmy moved around in his seat, but he didn't drink from his right away.

Instead, he said, "So tell me about you, man. What was Vegas like?"

I took a pull on my beer. "It's big. Let me tell you. There're big changes in the wind out there. It's starting to grow like crazy. Even before I went inside, you could smell the changes coming. By the year 2000, it's not even going to be the same town. A lot of the old casinos are closing up. The Landmark, the Silver Slipper, a few others...they even tore a couple of them down."

"The Landmark? Isn't that the one that looks like a giant mushroom sticking up out of the ground?"

"That's the one. It was only around twenty years old when they brought it down."

"Man, why do they want to destroy those places?"

"To build bigger ones. I hear that eventually all the older casinos are gonna go. The Sands, the Dunes, the Desert Inn, all of them."

His chestnut-colored eyes widened into the look of someone who is just now learning that there is a complete world out there beyond Big Pine Key.

"I heard about those places. I gotta get out there one of these days. The action is still great, though, isn't it?"

"It's still great," I said dryly, "and I ought to know because I contributed more than my share to it."

Shimmy showed surprise on his baby-face. "You? Man, I didn't know that. What...what..."

"I never could pass by the dice tables with money in my pocket."

"Dice. Shit, that's a tough game, brother."

"Not if you know how to play it. What's tough is when you've got twenty or thirty thousand spread around the table and the shooter sevens out on you. Poof. There it all goes, right down the toilet."

He relaxed back into the booth, running a hand through thick, black hair.

"Man, I'll stick to poker. With that game, you only have to beat the other players, not the house. At least you got a shot, and if you're a good player, you can be a favorite to win."

I'd heard all of these arguments before. Shimmy wasn't really arguing, he was just trying to tell me in a very indirect way that I have a problem I should do something about, because it's cost me a lot of money.

Thing was, I already knew all that. Even though I

was smart enough to know better, I still somehow wanted to believe, deep down, that the big score was waiting for me at some dice table somewhere.

He ordered up another beer.

"So what'd you have working out there?"

"A lot of things. Up until the diamond deal, I was doing all kinds of things."

"Like what?"

"Well, for example, I had this mail order thing going. Selling those books that aren't really books, but rather, places to store cash and valuables. You know, cut-out inside where the pages are." I held my hands out like an open book.

"Oh, like you see in the movies."

"Right. I got about twenty-five bucks apiece for them. But I had a deal with this second-story guy I knew. Guy they call Doctor Chicago. One of the top cat burglars in the country. Broken in to over a thousand homes, never been caught. I mean, he gets past alarms and guard dogs and the whole bit."

"How's he manage that?"

"I don't know how he does it. Anyway, he paid me a grand for the name and address of each customer, then he would go to their home, wait for them to leave, slip in and look for the book. Every one of those books was loaded. Jewels, Rolexes, cash...fucking loaded. All of them."

"You just sold him the addresses? That's it?"

"That's it. I sell him the address, he takes all the risk. I cleared about ninety grand when all was said and done. But he made over a million."

Shimmy smiled through glistening white teeth. "He'd go wherever these people lived? Anywhere in the country?"

"Sure. Even with the travel expenses, it was worth it to him. He said some of his biggest scores were in tiny little apartments in rundown parts of hick towns. People who didn't trust banks, or –"

"Or people like us. Members of the cash economy."

We both had a good chuckle.

As we clicked our bottles together, the hazy outlines of a plan floated into my mind.

SIXTEEN

It was dark out by the time I left Mambo's. High clouds blacked out the moon. Looking down the silent street toward Truman a few blocks away, I could see traffic flowing in both directions.

As I headed that way, a car pulled up to a stop next to me.

I braced for trouble.

"Don Roy Doyle?" said the driver. He spoke across the front seat through a lowered passenger-side window.

I kept on walking.

"Doyle?" he repeated as the car slid past me. He jumped out, flashing a badge. "FBI. Hold it right there."

He got out, then came around to the sidewalk.

"Hands on the car," he said. "Come on, you know the routine."

He patted me down. When he was satisfied, he

said, "Get in the car."

I looked at him. Khaki pants, a bright yellow Hawaiian shirt, worn outside to conceal the waistband holster.

The "new" FBI.

J Edgar Hoover would be rolling over in his grave, puking his guts up.

"What's the beef?" I asked.

"Just get in, Doyle. And don't try anything."

I got in the passenger side. He drove me to a spot I remembered from my childhood.

It was abandoned now, much worse for the wear, but when I was a kid, I remembered the bakery that used to be there, not far from my house, in fact. The aromas that flowed endlessly from that building were some of my favorite memories of growing up. For some reason, no other bakery ever smelled as good.

My mother would buy Cuban bread in there every day, then when she could afford it, she'd bring me a few cookies or other treats. Often times, on my way home from school, I would detour just to pass by that great old building, inhaling its pleasures.

Now, however, it sat empty, crumbling, ready to surrender.

He escorted me inside. Reaching over to the side wall, he flipped a light switch which looked like it had been recently rigged up. It lit up a naked bulb suspended from the high ceiling.

All remnants of the bakery had disappeared, with dirt and junk everywhere. Under the bulb sat an old, cleaned-off wooden desk with three chairs around it.

He nudged me into one of them, but remained standing himself.

"All right, here we are in your little playground. So who the hell are you and what's going on here?" I asked.

He showed his badge again. This time I took a closer look.

"I'm Special Agent Ryder," he said. "I understand you've been having some trouble with former mayor Whitney."

I had to laugh. Is there anything in this town that isn't public knowledge?

"What of it?"

"What of it? Oh, nothing much."

He finally sat down in the chair behind the desk and continued. "Only that I know he's guilty of just about every crime imaginable over the last thirty years, including whacking your pal Sullivan. This local jerk, Ortega, he's trying to pin that on you, but you and I both know who did it. Whitney's got a date with justice, and I intend to see that he keeps it."

I stood up to leave. "You're full of sh—"

He quickly moved around the desk, shoving me back into the chair.

"You're not leaving until I say so."

For a guy who was only medium build, he had giant-sized balls. It was just the two of us there in that dark old building and I could've cracked his skull right then and there for pushing me down in that chair. But he was a fed, and there was no percentage in it whatsoever.

I sat there and took it.

"What the hell is this shit?" I said. "If this was a real FBI roust, we'd be in your office, not in some falling-down building with the rats and lizards."

Ryder said, "I'm FBI all right, Doyle. You can bet on that."

"Then what're we doing here? In this place?"

I took another look at our surroundings. The light bulb cast a harsh glare across the desk. Not that it mattered, since there was only an ashtray on it. Beyond the desk, shadows gave way to total darkness.

"Let's just say this is a...a...let's call it an unofficial discussion. A fine example of a dedicated federal law enforcement officer working overtime, after hours, in a secret meeting with a Confidential Informant. All in the name of truth, justice, and the American way."

"Informant, my ass. Why should I do anything to help you?"

He came around to sit on the front of the desk, just a foot or two away from me. This close, I could see he appeared to be in excellent shape. His body was relaxed.

"You're looking at it backwards," he said. *I'm* here to help *you*. Unless I miss my guess, you're going after Whitney on your own. If for no other reason than to get out from under this murder frame."

He pulled a cigarette out of the pack in his shirt pocket, sparking it with a Bic lighter, whose flame shot up about a foot into the air.

Then he went on. "But you may need a little boost here and there. A little help from an unseen hand. That's where I come in. I can give you the FBI."

I looked hard at him, figuring him to be in his early thirties. His face told me he was deadly serious.

"Why? Why would you want to get me out of a murder charge? It's not even a federal beef."

He began to gesture with his hands. They were clear gestures, easy to read, and they complemented his words.

"You know a lot of people in this town, Doyle. The kind of people who might have the information I want. The kind of people who wouldn't tell me shit."

"What kind of information?"

"We think Whitney's in bed with the Russian mob. We also think they're down here establishing a base to move into Cuba when Castro gives up. Probably to set up gambling and prostitution operations. We're not sure of the details just yet."

I sat still while he got up to walk around, burning energy.

"Like I said, Doyle, you name the crime, Whitney's done it. But we don't have a shred of evidence on him, especially for federal offenses. So I can't touch him, yet. However, if a private citizen—yourself, for example—should suddenly get the urge to dig something up on him, well...I'd certainly do what I could to grease the way. Unofficially, of course."

"Yeah, but the FBI doesn't act 'unofficially'. What's your real reason?"

"I just told you. Anything else is my business. Now are you ready to cooperate?"

"What's to keep me from just blowing off the whole thing and skipping town? Which I've got half a mind to do anyway."

He threw the cigarette hard onto the concrete floor, stomping on it.

"Because if you do, there will be a warrant issued for your arrest. You will be hunted down and arrested for an armed robbery that will have taken place, an armed robbery for which you will have no credible alibi, and one in which you will have been positively identified by two eyewitnesses. That, plus the obvious violation of your parole, which requires you to maintain weekly visits with your parole officer, would mean a fifteen-to-twenty-year stretch, minimum. You ready for that?"

I didn't answer. But I think he picked up the "no" in my eyes.

He lowered his voice a notch, losing the bad-cop hard edge. "Look, Doyle. I know you better than you think I do. I know you've been on the grift for a long time. You stood up for Sullivan, and did your bit out in Nevada, *and* you kept your mouth shut. I know you don't work with cops, especially the FBI. But I'm not like any other cop."

I was beginning to believe him.

He said, "Get us anything you can on Whitney's link to the Russians."

He leaned closer toward me, slipping a scrap of paper into my shirt pocket.

"This's my private phone number. I've got one of those new cellular phones you carry around with you, so you can get me twenty-four hours a day."

Then, he shifted his voice all the way down to a

cold, hard whisper. "Whitney's nothing but scum. He's going down. One way...or another. You get my meaning?"

I got it, all right. I threw him a nod. Our meeting was over.

MIKE DENNIS

SEVENTEEN

The next day, I found Milton shooting pool in a smoky little joint behind one of the shopping centers on North Roosevelt. His long hair flowed out from beneath a soft-brim hat, which tried real hard to cover up a heavy bandage.

He was bent over the table, lining up the seven ball for an easy long shot. The eight and the nine were cripples, hanging on the lips of their respective pockets.

I reached beneath my shirt to adjust my piece in my rear waistband, just in case I needed it, then moved over to a point a few feet off the table, directly in his line of vision.

As soon as he saw me fill up the background behind the seven, he stroked the cue ball, scuffing it with a loud, awkward clack. It rolled harmlessly off to the right.

"Nice shot, Milton," I said. "Real finesse. You got

136

this game down."

He came up to me. "What do you want?"

"I heard you were a world-class pool player. I just wanted to see an exhibition. You know, the game as it was meant to be played."

Meanwhile, his opponent sank the seven, eight, and nine in quick fashion, scooping up the two twenty-dollar bills that lay on the table's rail. Another player stepped in to challenge the winner, throwing down a twenty of his own.

Milton went over to the wall to rack his cue. He grabbed his half-full bottle of beer, then swigged from it, hoping I would go away. I didn't.

"Now, we can move over to the corner here and speak privately, like gentlemen," I told him softly, "or I can reopen that gash on your healing head. What's it gonna be?"

Without comment, he walked toward the corner of the bar. I was right on his tail.

We took two stools at the far end. He was about my size, but as I'd learned from our previous meeting, not nearly as tough as he should've been.

Apprehension crept into his eyes. "What do you want, Doyle? Why you bothering me?"

"Let's just say I don't appreciate being grabbed off the street. Especially not by the likes of you."

"Yeah, well...you already made that point." His hand gestured toward the bandage on his head. "So now what do you want."

"I want to know how Frankie Sullivan wound up down on Front Street the other night with his throat cut."

"Hey! That wasn't me. I had no part of that."

He pulled nervously from his beer, nearly draining it.

"Oh, I know you didn't do it, Milton. You don't have what it takes for a job like that. But I just bet you have a good idea who the old man sent out to do it."

"I don't know nothing about it."

His eyes darted up and down the beer bottle, over to the pool table, and anywhere else he could think of so he wouldn't have to look at me.

"Who was it, Milton? Was it your playmate Bradley?"

"I told you I don't know nothing! Bradley works hand-in-glove with Mr Whitney. They don't tell me shit."

He finished his beer and signaled for another. Moments later, it was there.

"Well, why don't you get him to tell you?"

"Hmph! Yeah, right."

I kept my voice down in the polite zone. "Yes,

Milton. Really. You can find out what happened. You and Bradley are tight, aren't you?"

"Yeah, we're tight, Doyle. And that means I'm not snitchin' him to *you*." He started in on his fresh beer.

"Milton, I just want to know who did it. After all, I'm not a cop. For all I know, Bradley didn't do it."

"He didn't. So leave it alone!"

"I thought you said you didn't know. That they never tell you anything. And now you say he didn't do it."

He went for his beer again, but I grabbed it, slamming it down on the bar, hard.

"Hey, fuck you, Doyle! That's all I know. Bradley didn't have—"

I wrapped my hand around his index finger and bent it back, way back. He winced. I bent it back a little farther, raising his pain level.

"Listen, asshole," I whispered. "I want to know who clipped Sullivan. If you don't want to tell me, this finger goes, right now. If you make a peep in here or draw any attention to us, I'll crack your fucking arm in two, I swear to God. Sullivan's dead and my money's gone, so I've got nothing to lose, Milton. You understand me?"

He nodded while trying not to scream.

I kept up the pressure.

139

"Tell me!"

His free hand went palm down, telling me he had enough. He tried to say "okay" but it wouldn't come out.

I loosened my grip on his finger, but didn't let go entirely. He exhaled out all of the sharp pain, but the heavy soreness stayed with him.

He finally caught his breath, speaking between gasps, "Bradley didn't do it. But he farmed it out to two guys from Lauderdale."

That would figure. No direct connection to the old man.

"Who were they?"

"Hey, what's the dif—"

I grabbed the finger again, bending it to the point of snapping. Milton's upper body wrenched in pain.

But I had to hand it to him, he kept quiet.

"Awright, *awright!*"

I let go. He massaged his finger but it didn't do him much good.

"Yuri. Yuri Vasiliev. That's the only name I know, but he's Bradley's contact up there."

"Vasiliev? Is he Russian?"

"Yeah."

"Who is he?"

"How the fuck should I know?" he replied.

I went for the finger, but he pulled his hand back fast.

"Hey!" he said. "That's all I know. You want the guy's life story, call his mother."

I flagged down the bartender. "Give my friend here another cold one," I said. He brought the beer. I threw a five on the bar.

I looked back at Milton.

"You were a good boy today. You deserve a drink on me."

I headed for the door, but he called after me. "Doyle!" I turned back to him. He was still rubbing his finger and his hand. "That...that girlfriend of yours..."

I was back on him in an eyeblink, grabbing his shirt collar. "What did you say?"

"I...well...I just..."

"*Give.*"

I took his head between my big hands, ready to crush him to dust.

"I just don't go along with hurting women, you know what I mean? So I'm telling you...Bradley...he's capped the deal with this Yuri guy. Your girlfriend's next."

"What?"

"You heard me. But you didn't get it from me, you understand? I'm just telling you 'cause I don't think it's right. Hurting women, I mean."

I grabbed his shirt front, then shook him once. Hard.

It was all I could do to control my fury. "Why does Whitney want to kill her? She doesn't know anything. She's no threat to him at all."

He rubbed his wrist, then his forearm. I could tell the soreness was creeping up toward his elbow. I shook him so hard, he wheezed his answer.

"Bradley tells me you pissed the old man off the other day. Icing the girl is his way of getting back at you."

Before he finished his sentence, I was out the door.

SETUP ON FRONT STREET

EIGHTEEN

I raced back to Norma's.

On the way, I realized what was going on. I got under Whitney's skin, all right, like no one else had probably done in a long time. He could see I wasn't afraid of Ortega, that I wasn't going to take any of this sitting down.

Only problem was, he couldn't kill me as long as the frame for Sully's murder was holding. If I went down for it, that put him in the clear. So it figured that Norma had to go as my punishment for getting uppity with him.

Running from the car to her apartment building, then up two flights of stairs, I pulled my .22 as I ran down the hallway toward her apartment. Everything looked okay, but I clung to the wall as I neared the door.

I heard the radio playing inside. Country music,

Norma's favorite. Slowly, I reached for the doorknob, turning it, pushing the door back an inch at a time. The music became clearer — a Merle Haggard weeper.

When I got the door all the way open, I peered inside. I could only see into the living room. Nothing out of order.

I edged my way in, both hands on my gun. From my left, a figure darted out of the kitchen, startling me.

"Hi, honey."

It was Norma.

I let out a huge exhale. Replacing the gun into my waistband, I took her in my arms.

"You scared the shit out of me, you know that?" I said.

"Why? What's — the gun — why did you have your gun out?"

I pulled myself together quickly.

"Has anyone been here? Anyone at all?"

"No. Why?"

"Any phone calls? Anything out of the ordinary?"

"No, nothing...well...there was a phone call a few minutes ago, but that wasn't — "

"Who? *Who was it?*" I shook her.

"Stop it! You're — "

I stopped.

"Who *was* it?"

Her eyes regained that innocence I remembered from so long ago. The look I carried around in my head during my years in the joint.

"It was only the building manager."

"What'd he want?"

"He said there was an electrical problem or something—oh, I don't know, something about circuit breakers—and that he was sending two electricians up to take care of it. He wanted to make sure I'd be here to let them in."

I grabbed her hand, pulling her toward the door.

"We're out of here."

She resisted, slowing me down.

"Don Roy! What's going on? What's this all about?"

I kept moving, dragging her behind me until she finally caught up. We took the stairs down. I held her back as I scoped out the parking area. No movement anywhere, so we made a break for the car.

Fortunately, her apartment complex was laid out in a pretty confusing manner. Poorly-marked buildings, out-of-the-way entrances, parking lots all over the place created a real hodge-podge. Anyone coming here for the first time would have a lot of trouble finding their way around.

Once we got the car going, I told her, "We can't stay at your place. *You* can't stay there."

"Why not? What's happening?"

"There are men who are after y—after me. I can't tell you any more than that, but please believe me, we're not safe there. We've got to stay somewhere else for a while."

As we headed down the exit road, I glimpsed the rear view mirror. A dark blue Land Rover circled one of the buildings, the driver invisible behind dark tinted windows.

I took her straight to her mother's up on Big Coppitt Key.

I know she was thinking I might've been afraid back there. I was afraid all right, but not of Vasiliev or his pals. I was afraid that I'd've shot them right there in her apartment the second they walked through the door.

Gunfire, naturally, would bring the cops. Once I put weapons into the Russians' dead hands, it probably would've gone down as self-defense, but just having the gun in my possession was a violation of my parole. Ortega would've seen to it that I was sent back.

I couldn't have that.

NINETEEN

I took it easy all the way through the ten-mile trip back to town from Big Coppitt. The calm breeze drifting in the open window settled me down to the point where I could check out my options.

One, I could corner Bradley the way I'd done with Milton. Maybe do him in at the same time.

But that wouldn't accomplish anything. Bradley was probably not as much of a pushover as Milton was. It could get real rough. What's more, I doubted that he could tell me anything I didn't already get from Milton.

Besides, wasting him would permanently erase any link between Sully's killers and Whitney.

Two, I could confront Whitney with what I knew, hoping to rattle him and push him into making a big mistake.

But if he kept his cool, which was certainly possible, then he'd never stop until he got me.

On the other hand, if I also took option number

one, putting Bradley down first, the old man would lose his buffer to the Russians. Then he might not want to involve himself in such a direct way.

Possible, but too many ways to go wrong.

Three, I could tell Ryder what I knew, and let the FBI work it out, nailing Vasiliev and Whitney in the process.

Out of the question. They might get Bradley, maybe even Vasiliev, but even if they both rolled over, which was far from certain, Whitney might well beat the rap. His money and connections around here ran deep. Very deep.

Besides, never trust the government to do anything on your behalf, especially if you've got a lot at stake.

Four, I had to remember one thing: I wanted my two hundred thousand.

It had cost me three years of my life and I came all the way back here to get it. Plus, I had a feeling Sully died for it.

***

As soon as I got back to town, I went straight to the rooming house I stayed in when I first got back to town. I damn sure couldn't go back to Norma's, so the room would have to do for the time being.

Also, I needed to stash my piece again. I had things

to do in broad daylight that didn't require a gun, so I couldn't risk being picked up with it.

After I ditched the weapon, I went out again, this time on foot, over to Keys Tees.

Avi was hustling a customer into some expensive T-shirt add-ons when I walked in. The guy was resisting for all it was worth, but after a few minutes of Avi's perfect-pitch pressure, he caved and handed over his plastic.

Avi bagged the merch, the sucker left, then we were alone.

"Donny, my boy!" He wasn't smiling. "So sorry to hear about your good friend Sullivan. I been in his bar. He was good businessman."

"Yeah, well, not that good, apparently."

"I hear they think you do it, but I know different. You and he good friends."

Is there anything that ever happens in this town without everyone knowing about it?

"Listen, Avi. What do you know about a guy named Yuri Vasiliev?"

His dark eyes were still, but the lids flickered ever so slightly. I wouldn't've caught it if I wasn't looking right into them.

"Who?" He tried hard to stay cool.

"Yuri Vasiliev. Come on, you heard me."

149

"Nothing," he replied. "I don't know the name."

"Avi, don't bullshit me now. Who is he?"

"I don't know —"

I took one step toward him, menace all over my face.

"Donny, wait." He held up a hand between us. "You don't know this guy. You don't *want* to know him."

"Let me pick my own friends, Avi. Now, who is he?"

Reflexively, he looked around. It was just the two of us. He gripped my forearm, pulling me to the back of the store.

Once we were in the far corner, he hunched his shoulders a little. His eyes were anxious and he spoke in hushed tones, as if he were about to reveal nuclear secrets.

"Where you get his name from, Donny?"

"An invitation list to the White House."

"I'm in trouble if they know I tell you anything." His voice was hollow with fear.

"They'll never know. Now tell me."

He reached into his pocket for a handkerchief. After dabbing at his forehead a couple of times, he used it on his palms. They needed it.

"He's bad guy. Very bad. He is number one

enforcer for the Russians in Fort Lauderdale. Sent down two years ago from Brighton Beach."

Brighton Beach, up in Brooklyn. I knew about it. Center of operations for the Russian mob in the United States and a direct line to the old country. This guy Vasiliev was obviously a heavyweight.

"What's his connection down here?"

I already knew it was Whitney, of course, but I wanted to see if Avi could tell me anything about it.

"I don't know of any."

"Well, he must have one because he's here in town right now."

Avi's eyes widened. He checked the front of the store again to make sure no one was listening.

After another dab or two at his forehead, he said, "Yuri Vasiliev is *here?* In Key West?"

The fear wouldn't leave his face.

"I don't know if he's *still* here, but he was out driving around the Ocean Walk apartments forty-five minutes ago. Now, what's up with this guy, Avi? Why're you pissing your pants?"

"Donny, you must try to understand. I never see him before. I only hear about him. All bad things. He deals in death. If he is in town, someone is going to die. And if he knew I was talking about him like this, I would be that someone."

"Don't worry. I told you, no one's gonna know. Now, there's one more thing. Do you know of any connection between Vasiliev and Wilson Whitney?"

"*Whitney?* Who used to be mayor?"

Avi couldn't hide his astonishment that the two might be linked.

"Yeah, him."

"No, none. Does *he* know Vasiliev?"

"I'm pretty sure. Or at least one of his goons knows him."

"You must believe me, Donny. I know nothing of Whitney. I pay him bribe once, it was back around eighty-five, eighty-six, during his last years as mayor. Just to get police to stop undercover work in my store. I see him ten minutes, no more. Nothing since."

His voice got softer and softer till I could barely hear him. It was as though he thought there were hidden microphones all over the store.

Hell, maybe there were. Who knows how these people operate?

I went along with it, whispering, "So, what you're saying is this Vasiliev's a real badass."

"What I am saying is, if he is in town, it must be important. *Very* important. He is their best and he reports only to the top guys. If you are involved in this, Donny, you must be very, very careful."

152

SETUP ON FRONT STREET

He clutched my wrist for effect.
I gently removed his hand.
"Thanks for the warning, Avi."
I left the store.

TWENTY

I don't carry a wallet. Well, that's not exactly true.

I carry one whenever I'm holding fake ID, which is most of the time. This way, when I use a phony credit card, the mark sees me pull it out of a wallet, just like any other citizen would do. But wallet or no wallet, I always carry my money around in a clip, in my front pants pocket.

So right now, until Yale Lando has my ID ready, I have no wallet.

This means I carry everything else around in my pockets. Normally, I don't mind until I have to find something other than keys or money, which I can identify by feel. For everything else, I have to empty my pockets, which is a royal pain in the ass.

So that's exactly what I did. Right outside Avi's, I fished through all that shit until I found the phone number Rita gave me the other day.

Fortunately, I kept it with me instead of leaving it at Norma's. It wouldn't be wise to go back there just yet.

I walked to the Atlantic end of Duval Street, back to the outdoor restaurant where I'd seen Rita a couple of days before. A languid breeze rolled in from the ocean. Tourists loitered on the beach.

Calmly, I stepped up to the pay phone by the entrance. I slid a quarter into the slot and I had her on the line.

"Don Roy! Hey, how nice to hear from you."

She sounded like she meant it. In fact, I could hear the smile in her voice.

"Yeah, listen. Can you meet me at that restaurant? You know, the one from the other day?"

"Well, I guess so. When would you—"

"Right now. I'm standing at a pay phone out in front of the place as we speak."

"Well, let's see...it's about quarter past three. At four-thirty I have to be at—"

"Rita, please."

She realized it was serious.

"Okay. Give me twenty minutes."

I shambled over to the restaurant, taking an outdoor table like I did the other day. Glancing at the beach, I saw there were more people there today, and they were more active.

A guy and girl in their early twenties raced in and out of the water, splashing, tackling each other. The way they rolled around on the sand reminded me of an old black-and-white movie I'd seen, but I couldn't remember the name.

A little farther away, a few kids, around nine or ten years old, squealed in delight over some game they were playing involving a big inflatable ball.

All the while, the breeze, that beautiful soft breeze, kept washing over me from the shore under sunlit skies.

Rita said twenty minutes? She made it in fifteen.

I saw her approach my table in some kind of two-piece belly-baring thing. She had my full attention, all right, as she sashayed toward me.

This time she greeted me by leaning in with a one-armed hug, accompanied by a peck on the cheek. For full effect, she made sure to rub her breasts up against me while nuzzling my face.

Subtlety was never her strong suit. I could see how she corralled BK.

"How are you doing today?" she murmured. "It's so good to see you again."

Even this close, I caught only a slight trace of perfume, but the trace was enough. I had to admit, it was intoxicating.

I wasn't too sure how to respond. I patted her shoulder as she was hugging me.

I said, "Fine," or something like it. Anyway, we sat down. I cleared my throat.

The fact was, though, I was clearing my head. I hoped she didn't spot it.

She ordered an iced tea. I was ready to open, but she jumped in first.

"I was really surprised to hear from you so soon. Actually, I wasn't sure I'd ever hear from you at all." She said this through an alluring smile.

I think I might've blushed right there, but only for a second. I didn't recall ever doing it before, because, you know, beautiful women never spoke to me that way, so I wasn't really sure what a blush was supposed to feel like. But I know my face warmed up a degree or two for sure.

I broke a small smile without thinking about it, then turned my head downward and to the right. I heard her suppress a giggle.

Finally, I said, "Well...thanks for coming."

Shit, how lame was that!

I needed a little more head-clearing time. Reaching for my tea glass, I took a long, long swig.

She lit a cigarette and waited for me to continue.

MIKE DENNIS

Once I collected myself, I said, "I asked you to come here because I need to know something. To your knowledge, does the old man—or BK, for that matter—know anyone who might be Russian?"

"Russian? You mean, like...from Russia?"

"Well, yeah."

"I don't, uh...I don't think so."

She took a drag off her cigarette to help her recall.

"You sure?"

She sank into thought. "I can't think of...oh, wait. A couple of months ago—no, it was longer than that...maybe around Christmas—this guy came to the house one night. He met with BK in the study. Later, BK introduced me to him. He was a foreigner, I remember. His name wasn't like anything I'd ever heard before, and he spoke with some kind of European accent."

"Was his name Vasiliev? Yuri Vasiliev?"

"No. That wasn't it. It was a real long name, it was like, uh, like...Chana—Charmo—oh, I can't even begin to say it. As I remember, it sounded like it might've been Russian, I guess. I can't say for sure. But he was definitely a foreigner. An older guy. Like around sixty."

"What did he and BK talk about?"

"I don't know. Like I said, they went into his study. They were in there about a half hour, then he left. I

158

never saw him again."

She turned slightly in her chair to face the breeze from the water, which had picked up some. It rustled her hair a little. I liked it.

I said, "And BK never told you anything about him? Or about what they discussed?"

"No. He didn't. But, you know, now that you mention Russia, back a couple of years ago, while you were away, BK did set up a sister-city deal with some Russian city."

My eyebrows went up.

"He did?"

"Yeah. It was one of the first things he did as mayor. Now that I think about it, a couple of Russians showed up on the island not long after that, in connection with the whole thing."

"Did BK ever go over there?"

"No, he could never get away. But..." Her voice lowered several tones as she realized what she was about to say. "But the old man went in his place."

I practically saw the light bulb click on over her head.

"Do you know where he went? What he did over there? Anything at all!"

It was all I could do to stay calm.

"No, no I don't. What's all this Russia stuff about,

anyway?"

She stubbed out the cigarette, then swallowed the last of her tea.

"I can't tell you right now, Rita. But listen, did BK or the old man have any dealings with Frankie Sullivan?"

"Not that I know of."

She looked around for the waitress. Once she found her, she signaled for a refill on the iced tea.

Then she said, "BK and I were in his bar a few times, and he and Sullivan seemed to know each other. I mean, beyond the local-businessman-knows-the-mayor kind of thing, you know? It seemed like they were more than casually acquainted, but I never knew anything about it."

"But BK never mentioned any deals with him? Or any connection between Sully and the old man?"

"No."

She reached for another cigarette. As she shook it loose from the pack, it fell out onto the concrete floor. She left it there, but didn't go for another one.

"Look, Don Roy, what're you getting at here?"

"Like I said, I can't tell you right now, 'cause I got nothing solid."

Her voice slipped into come-on mode, and so did her flashing eyes.

"Oh, I'll bet you've got something solid for me."

Her smile said even more than that. So did her soft hand as she lightly wrapped it around my index finger.

I chuckled.

"As nice as it sounds, the last thing we need right now is to get carried away with that."

I knew she agreed. I mean, she's the mayor's wife, for Chrissake. She finally let go of my finger.

I said, "Is there any way of finding out what the old man did while he was in Russia? Or if he had anything going with Sullivan?"

"Well, he might have something in his files. I know he has a hidden file cabinet in his office. He keeps all his real important stuff in there."

"Hidden cabinet?" My eyes snapped upward from my iced tea. "Where is it?"

"There's a big leather sofa against one wall. Right next to it is a boxy end table with a lamp on it. The table's the cabinet. The files are inside it."

I remembered the sofa. A big, heavy leather thing. Part of a corner set, with a matching armchair. The table was between them, right in the corner, blocked from view on all sides. Only the lamp was visible, sticking up from it.

Pretty clever, keeping it right in plain sight.

"Do you know what's in it?"

"No, but I've seen him a couple of times move the chair out of the way and open it. From what I could tell, there were just files in there."

I looked around to make sure no one was paying attention.

"How does he open it?"

"It's got a lock on it and he uses a key. Like opening the front door to a house."

"Does BK have something like that, too?"

"Not really. We have a safe, but it's just for cash and jewelry...that kind of thing. The old man keeps stuff in there, too."

"He does?"

"Yeah. We live in his house in Old Town, the one he lived in for so many years before he moved out to Key Haven. Way back when, he had a safe built into the floor inside one of the closets. He's got one in Key Haven, too. He uses them both."

"Both?"

"Right. But he keeps all his important legal papers and shit in that file cabinet. Right in his office, where he can get to them when he needs them."

"Do you know what he's got in the closet safe in your house?"

"Uh-uh. That one has two compartments inside it. One for BK and me, and one for him. Each compartment has its own key and he's got his."

I ran that around the block.

Then I said, "Listen, do you know if he's going out of town anytime soon?"

"I know he's leaving on April sixteenth. Him and his bimbo girlfriend."

"April sixteenth? How is it you've got the date down?"

"He goes over to the Bahamas for a few days every year right after paying his income taxes. Probably to celebrate how much he saved by cheating."

I let out a big exhale as I sat back in my chair. After a moment, I stood up, throwing a five on the table.

"I've got to go now, but I owe you one."

She grabbed my arm. "Don Roy, does this mean we're going to get that old bastard?"

"No it doesn't. And don't get your hopes up. Remember, he's no small-time punk."

"Well...if that's the case, then..." She gave me that pouty smile again. "Then can't a girl get her hopes up about somethin?"

I smiled goodbye back at her.

On my way out, my smile turned into a chuckle.

TWENTY-ONE

Outside the restaurant, I went back to the pay phone. As soon as Rita left, I dropped a bunch of coins into the slot and dialed the Vegas number.

After a couple of rings, Doctor Chicago picked up.

"Doc. Don Roy Doyle."

"Don Roy, my man! What's happenin'? You out now?"

"Been out over a week now. I'm back in Key West doing my parole. Glad to see you're still in Vegas."

"Oh man, I'd have to be crazy to leave this place. Pickin's here are so-o-o easy. Motherfuckers just leave shit lyin' around, waitin' for me to come along and pick it up. Just like always."

"Amazing, isn't it?" I said. "How Vegas is really changing, but some things just stay the same."

It really was amazing. Hotels in Vegas, like everywhere else, were switching to those new card-type keys that slip into a slot. But Doc could get past them as though the doors to the rooms were wide open.

"Yeah, man. You right. So, what you got goin' down there?"

I turned around to face the big, blue ocean. Looking at its gentle waves sent a calm swell over me.

"Yeah, well, that's why I called you. I got a job I need done, and you're the man to do it."

"Shi-it! Lemme hear it. Whatchu got?"

"It's a house here in Key West. I'm interested in the contents of a particular file cabinet."

"What kind of cabinet?"

"Mickey Mouse. Disguised as an end table with a dead bolt lock. Opens with a regular key."

"Shit man, that sounds like somethin' you could handle yourself."

"The cabinet's nothing," I said, "but getting into the house might be difficult. Alarms, plus there's a maid living there."

"When we talkin' about?"

"Okay, today's the third. The owner'll be leaving town on the sixteenth. After that, you've got a three-day window of opportunity."

"The sixteenth? Lessee, that's...that's a week from Tuesday. Okay, man. The Doctor is *in!* I'll be there."

"Yeah, but Doc, look. I know what your fee is for

these custom jobs, and I'm kind of strapped right now. I can—"

"Whoa! Don Roy, you my man! You put me on to some pretty serious scores back a few years ago with them phony books that you keep money in."

"Well, you paid me for each one of those. I mean, I—"

"No, no, no. I owe you one, man. Just get me a plane ticket and this one'll be on the house."

"Hey man, you serious? That'd really mean a lot to me."

"Serious as a fuckin' heart attack, man! Shit, all you want's some files in a regular house? Say no more! They're yours!"

"Thank you, brother. I'll send you the plane ticket. Same PO box?"

"The very same. See you in Key West, man."

I reached in my pocket for another quarter. Ryder's number looked back at me from the scrap of paper he gave me.

This was a first for me. Calling the FBI.

Out of instinct, I hesitated, but dialed the number anyway.

His voice was relaxed, much more than mine.

"Ryder, this is Doyle."

"What's up?"

"Whitney Senior went to Russia a couple of years back. Can you find out where he went over there and what he did?"

"Hmm...passport and travel records. That's State Department stuff."

I felt the government stonewall going up.

I said, "Who gives a shit? Can you find out or can't you?"

"Why would he go to Russia?"

"BK arranged a sister-city deal with some town over there, and the old man went as the official rep of Key West."

He paused. Finally, he said, "I'll see what I can do."

"Wait a minute. There's a couple of other things. First, I need what you've got on a guy named Yuri Vasiliev. He's Russian muscle."

"I know him. We've got a jacket on him. What else?"

"Sully told me he gave some money to one of those outfits that invest your money for you...what do you call it..."

"Investment counselor."

"Yeah, that's it. He said he invested, uh, some of the profits from his club with these people. You know, where the money goes into office buildings and whatnot. I think that might have something to do with all this. Can you find out anything about it?"

"Doyle, that's SEC shit. The FBI doesn't have jur — "

"Wait a minute. What'd you call it?"

"SEC. The Securities and Exchange Commission. They're a very independent agency and they don't give out information to just anyone."

"Yeah, but you're not just anyone, right? You're FBI."

He groaned. "You don't understand. I can't go through official channels here. This is all off the record, what we're doing. I can't just call up the SEC and demand — "

"Listen, you were the one who dragged me to that fucking falling-down bakery, telling me how you could help."

"All right, now you listen. I want Whitney, just like you do. It's just not going to be easy, is all. I know a couple of people over at State, and maybe I can get a favor out of one of them. The SEC thing, well...I don't know."

"Well, do what you gotta do. Just remember, my life is on the line here!"

"Okay." He let out a sigh. "But it might take me a week or so."

"Shit, you can't get it any sooner?"

"Hey, I'm not a magician! Now, the Vasiliev

material, that's FBI. I can get it today. This other shit'll take time."

I muttered a curse before giving him the number of the rooming house. "Make it quick."

TWENTY-TWO

Over the next week, I kept a low profile, or at least as low as it gets in this town. Which means I walked back and forth from my rooming house to Mambo's every day, using side streets.

Ortega managed to spot me on the street a couple of times and patted me down for no good reason, just like he'd seen real cops do on TV. He always made sure to tell me that they were working around the clock to build a case against me. Then he added how much he was going to enjoy leading me away in handcuffs.

As big of an asshole as he was, I didn't think he was in Whitney's pocket. He really took all that cop shit seriously and didn't strike me as the kind who could be easily bought.

It was Wednesday, April tenth—all this cop talk, I sound like Joe Friday myself. Actually, I mentioned the date because a week had gone by with nothing from

Ryder.

He was looking more and more like a dead end.

Anyway, I was in Mambo's early that evening enjoying a little *ropa vieja* with yellow rice and black beans. Mambo insisted on feeding me, saying I hadn't been eating right since I got back home. And he was right.

He had the best yellow rice in town, I mean the very best. In Key West, with authentic Cuban restaurants all over the place, that's saying a lot. The kernels were always, always separate, bursting with flavor.

I drank the last of my beer right at the end of the meal.

The place was dead, according to the empty pool table and only one other occupied booth. A couple of guys sat at the bar with their backs to me, watching the baseball game. Mambo finished with some bolita business, then came out of the back room. On his way to my booth, he caught the waiter's eye.

"*¡Eduardo! ¡Dos cervezas!*"

Eduardo brought the beers and we sank into heavy conversation. I told him everything that happened since my return, all about Whitney, BK, Norma, and the Russians. The only part I left out was the FBI shakedown.

171

Not that Mambo would worry about the FBI, since he was strictly local, but I just didn't think he needed to know about it.

Besides, how would it look? Me, a career street guy, cozying up to the goddamn federals. I could hardly believe it myself.

Mambo absorbed the whole story. He leaned back in the booth and took another hit from his beer. Then he pulled a Cohiba from his pocket, examining it for a moment.

The cigar apparently consumed his thoughts for a few seconds. He toyed with it, rolling it around between his palms and twirling it between his fingers like a magician. He decided against lighting it for the time being, so he left it on the table, still in its wrapper.

"My brother," he said in Spanish, "I have to tell you that I have heard through my family that Wilson Whitney is very upset with you. You must be careful. *El tiene mucho poder.*"

Whenever Mambo heard something "through his family", you knew it was serious.

I replied, "I know he's powerful. And I've heard he's not too thrilled with me. But he's after Norma, me entendés?"

"The word is you interfered with BK's arrangement with her. And you also insulted Whitney in his home.

That really pissed him off, from what I hear."

"Well, why, then, does he bring the top Russky hitman in the entire fucking country down here to dust Norma? His own goons can't do it? I mean, we're small potatoes, right? *Fue solo un insulto pequeño.* So what's the big deal? Why all the high-priced firepower?"

Mambo finally surrendered to the temptation of the Cohiba. He unwrapped it, then clipped the tip.

After going through his sniffing and lighting routine, he finally said through a cloud of smoke, "*Para mandarte un mensaje.*"

"Send me a message? What message?"

"To make you think that killing both Sullivan and Norma was in response to your meeting with Whitney."

He puffed on his cigar, but I could tell he had more to say. I let him go on.

"I think Sullivan was killed for another reason altogether. And you came back to town at the right time, conveniently, to take the blame."

He took another big puff on the cigar, watching the smoke trail off to his right, toward the deserted pool table.

"*¿Por qué, Mambo?* Why was Sully killed?"

He contemplated that one for a minute. I could tell he was thinking of the right way to put it as he swigged from his beer bottle.

He carefully placed his Cohiba in a big ceramic tray.

"The Russian mafia is making preparations to bring their enterprise to Cuba once Castro goes. I mean everything. Drugs, prostitution, gambling, government corruption, everything. They've made a deal with Whitney to establish their base here in Key West using his influence, his real estate connections. Owning him, in other words. I think Sullivan got in the way somehow."

"Sully? He had no interest in the Russians. How was he in the way?"

"Maybe they wanted the building his bar was in. I don't know. But it was enough to get him killed. The Russians consider Key West a very important point of departure into Cuba. When Castro goes, they're positive they can move right across the straits and set up shop there without any problem. You know, because they're Russians, and because the Soviet Union was in Cuba for so long."

A wry smile slid across his face.

"But they'd be wrong?" I asked.

"Dead wrong."

His smile now a shade wider, he said, "What they don't realize is that, after more than forty years under the communist bootheel, and with Russian domination of Castro that whole time, the Cuban people have had it with them. I'm not saying the Russians will be thrown out on their asses, but it's going to be very, very difficult for them."

"How do you know this, man?"

His voice lowered a little through the thick cigar smoke. "The Key West-Cuba connection is much stronger, much deeper than anything they could come up with. Much older, too. Older than the Soviet Union itself. *Tú sabes eso, mi hermano.* Key Westers and Cubans share a special bond."

I gave him a nod.

He went on: "Our peoples have intermingled back and forth across the straits for over a hundred and fifty years. What I mean is, the Russians aren't the only ones waiting for Castro to leave power."

Up at the bar, the two guys watching the baseball game became aroused over a big play at the plate. They started shouting at the TV.

Mambo continued, his voice hushed. "My family has been preparing for that day for years now. We go to Cuba at least once a month to meet with our family members over there."

"I remember they were doing that when I was growing up. In fact, I remember seeing you and your brother leave on your family's boat from over in Key West Bight."

He nodded. "We've spent years making the necessary arrangements with the right people, the younger people, who will be in positions of power in the post-Fidel era. We've arranged to get the first gaming licenses awarded, and we've got our choice of hotels. Not only that, we've already got the rights lined up to import many necessary products like meat, liquor, and a lot of the things the big hotels and casinos are going to need. By the time the Russians get there, we'll already be in place, and they'll have to face a population that is fed up with Russians altogether."

This guy never failed to amaze me. Him and his whole family.

We talked a little more, then he ended with the caution, "But I tell you again, the Russians are not to be taken lightly. *Ten mucho cuidado, mi hermano.*"

Mambo never tossed warnings around loosely. If he gave you the glare and told you to be careful, you better do it.

I left his place that night by the back door and returned to my rooming house, mostly by way of the little off-street lanes, staying in the shadows.

TWENTY-THREE

The ringing phone jarred me out of a sound sleep.

I picked up right before the second ring, mumbling something like a hello.

"Doyle," Ryder said, "meet me at the Casa Marina for breakfast in thirty minutes."

My eyes could barely open as I shook myself awake.

"What time is it?"

"Six-thirty."

"Jesus! What—what the hell are you doing calling—"

"Your government never sleeps, pal. Just get your ass up and get over to the Casa Marina."

"And what's with The Casa Marina? That's one of the swankiest hotels in town! What are you, pulling some kind of expense account scam?"

"This is no scam. I've got something for you."

"Oh, you've got something?" I rasped as I finally snapped into second gear. "Then you can give it to me someplace where we won't be seen by any of Whitney's friends who might well be having breakfast in the Casa Marina themselves. Hmph! Where the fuck do they find you guys, anyway?"

"Well...where do you suggest, then?"

"Try the Waffle House on North Roosevelt. Think you can handle that, hotshot?"

"Okay, okay. Just be there in thirty minutes."

***

There were the usual assortment of early morning types at the Waffle House, most of them slurping down coffee in order to catapult themselves into their day's work. No chance of encountering any of Whitney's crowd in here under the harsh fluorescent lighting.

Ryder was waiting for me. At least he had sense enough to take a booth in the back. I sat down and poured coffee from the pot on the table. Also on the table was his new cellular phone, sitting upright between us like a plastic statue.

"Where've you been?" I asked. "It's been over a week."

"I told you it would take time."

"Yeah, and in the meanwhile, Vasiliev is running around on the loose."

Ryder poured cream into his coffee, then stirred it slowly.

"How do you know that?"

"Never mind how I know. Before you get started, let me tell you what I've come up with."

He sat back. "Okay. Let's have it."

I drew a warm pull from my coffee.

"Whitney and the Russians are working together, just like you thought. The Russians want to move into Cuba when the Beard kicks off. They're cutting deals with Whitney to use Key West as a preliminary kind of base camp. And when they move into Cuba, they're bringing their whole operation with them. Not just girls and gambling, but drugs, the heavy weapons trade, corruption, and all the rest of it."

Ryder picked up on it, showing surprise in his eyes.

"Which means they're essentially looking to retake Cuba for themselves."

I didn't tell him about the DeLimas' plans to inconvenience the Russians. Instead, I stayed on topic.

"And I'm told that Sullivan was killed because he was in the way, although I don't know how."

"I might have some information on that."

179

He shoved his coffee cup out of the way to make room for his briefcase on the table. He opened it and out came a plain manila folder. "But first, let me show you this."

He opened the folder to reveal an eight-by-ten photo. "This is Vasiliev."

He handed the photo to me. I looked at the black-and-white surveillance picture of a youngish guy, maybe in his late twenties. He wore an expensive leather coat that came down to the middle of his thighs while he stood by a vehicle as if he were about to get into it. It was dark-colored.

A Land Rover.

Ryder moved that photo aside.

"And here's a closeup."

This was a tighter shot of his face. Not a mug shot, but one of him in a candid moment, like he posed for it with some other people at a party or somewhere. I could see blurry figures of other people in the background.

This close, I saw the beginnings of lines around his eyes and at the corners of his mouth; his one-sided struggle with time had begun. I revised my estimate of his age to be around thirty-five.

But there was no mistaking one thing.

He was a killer, all right.

Even though he was smiling in the picture, he had that same cold, vacant look in his eyes that I'd seen in so many other eyes before.

Ryder went on. "He's thirty-five years old. He came to this country a few years ago with the first real wave of Russian mobsters. They were the ones who'd bought their way out of the USSR during the last years of communism."

I'd heard about the fall of communism while I was inside, and the subsequent mass arrivals of the Russian gangsters on our shores.

He said, "Anyway, we don't quite have all the names and numbers yet, but we do know that this Vasiliev is one of the top shooters for the entire US branch of the mob. The big boys up in Brighton Beach sent him down to Fort Lauderdale a couple of years ago when they were getting their Broward County operation set up. He runs a little group of thugs who provide all the muscle, and he's constantly seen in the company of the mob bosses. They turn to him whenever they have contracts on important people. Like the guy who was running for Broward commission last time out."

Ryder looked at me like I should know the rest of the story. My blank face told him I didn't, so he rolled his eyes, vibing lots of impatience.

181

"You may remember this. The guy was a real reformer type. Law and order all the way. He saw the threat the Russians posed, and he promised to send 'em back to Mother Russia."

"It doesn't ring a bell."

"Well, one night he and his wife were snatched in a brightly-lit restaurant parking lot. Local cops found their body parts a few days later stuffed into two 55-gallon oil drums in a dump in Oakland Park."

You know, it's one thing to do somebody who needs doing, or who really deserves it. But this politician, all he apparently did was mouth off to get some attention. They all do that, for Chrissakes. I mean, that's what politicians were born to do.

A little slapping around would've shut him up.

But then, to chop up his *wife*.

"Okay," I said. "What about Whitney and his Russian trip?"

"That took me a little time. I had to call Washington. Like I told you, I have a friend over at State. He went to—"

"State?"

"The State Department, Doyle. You know? Like, where the Secretary of State works?"

"Oh-h-h," I said, pretending this was all a great revelation to me.

If he was going to wake me up with the damn chickens, I was at least going to get a laugh or two out of the deal.

"Anyway," he continued, "my friend at State, he works for the Assistant Secretary for European and Canadian Affairs, and he had to call a friend of his at the Special Issuance Agency for the—"

"Shit, Ryder! Enough of the government mumbo-jumbo. Just tell me what you've got."

I had to take a big coffee hit. His bureaucratic doubletalk was making the room spin right before my eyes.

He got indignant on me.

"Look, I went to a lot of trouble to get this. And I violated FBI regulations by going interdepartmental. So don't give me—"

"FBI regulations? You mean like our little chat the other night in that abandoned bakery? That was in line with FBI regulations? Did J Edgar include that in his training manual? Or that part about how you were gonna frame me for a stickup if I didn't help you get Whitney? Is that in the new FBI playbook?"

"Bullshit, Doyle. That was—"

I shut him up. "Don't be pulling that righteous shit on me, G-Man. We're not kidding anybody here. We both want the same thing, and we're both willing to step over the line to get it."

The waitress brought his breakfast, some kind of omelet with toast. She asked me if I wanted a menu. I was hungry, but I didn't want to break bread with this asshole.

I waved her off, then poured more coffee into the thick white cup in front of me.

Ryder didn't say anything for a minute or two. He started fiddling with the eggs on his plate, buttering his toast, that kind of thing. Eventually, he looked up from his food.

"Two years ago this month, Whitney Senior flew to Miami, then to New York to begin his international mission of good will. Records show he spent the night in New York, although he could've made an easy connection that afternoon on a Lufthansa flight to Moscow via Frankfurt. He stays at a medium-priced hotel out by Kennedy Airport, then takes the very same Lufthansa flight the next afternoon."

"Any proof he saw the Russians in New York?"

"No. But whatever his reason for staying, it may well have been because he wanted to be near Kennedy Airport...which is in Brooklyn."

"Which is the American home...of the Russian mob."

"Bingo." He seemed quite surprised that I knew

that. "So, the next day, Whitney flies to Moscow. He spends the night there, then on to Odessa the following morning. Now, Odessa isn't really in Russia. It's in Ukraine, but they all speak Russian there, because it used to be part of the old USSR, and Odessa just happens to be the headquarters for worldwide Russian organized crime. He's there in Odessa another day and a half, after which he makes the short flight down to the town of Sevastopol, on the Black Sea coast. That's the so-called sister city of Key West. He spends the afternoon shaking hands and cutting ribbons, then it's back to Odessa for two more days. Then, Moscow for another day, New York for a full day and night, then back home."

"In other words, a ten-day trip, all for a few hours in the sister city."

"Right."

He paused to take a bite of his food, which must've been getting cold by this time.

"Now, we don't have any record of who he saw or who he spoke with during his time in New York, Moscow, or Odessa, because we weren't tailing him. In fact, I'm damn lucky to have gotten this information at all. You know, Doyle, this stuff is really hard to come by, even within the government. All this happened during the Cold War, and there were strict regulations against—"

I put my hands to my ears.

"Spare me any more government bullshit. Please!"

"All right, all right."

He swirled some of his eggs around on the plate. They looked terrible. He apparently had the same idea because he didn't eat any more of them.

Instead, he pulled his cigarette pack out of his shirt pocket and shook one loose. He torched it with his Bic, set at flamethrower level.

"And that brings us to your friend Sullivan."

I felt myself bend forward in anticipation. I was sure, though, that he didn't catch it.

"What'd you find?"

"Well, I have to tell you that it took me several hours on the phone. I had to lean on this guy I know at the Treasury Department. I say I know him; actually, I barely know him. I really had to persuade him into helping me out. But he eventually steered me to the right person at the commissioners' office of the SEC, and let me tell you, that was no day at the beach. They shuttled me off to the Division of Investment Management. There, I got some twenty-one-year-old girl on the phone who put me through to the Bureau of—"

"*Ryder!*"

He flinched. "Hey! You were pretty impatient, mister, with all your talk about me taking so long to get this information. You have no idea what it takes."

"Alright already. So I have no idea. Cut to the chase."

He calmed down a little. So did I. He paused for the all-important dramatic effect while he puffed on his cigarette.

Do they teach these guys this shit at the FBI Academy?

"It may interest you to know that on May 3, 1989, more than a year after you went inside, Sullivan opened a rather large account with a Miami investment management firm. According to the Securities and Exchange Commission records, a little over four hundred thousand dollars, to be exact."

I'll be damned. So Sully was telling the truth after all.

"Go on," I said.

"It wouldn't surprise me if that figure coincided exactly with what you guys took down in that swindle out in Las Vegas."

"Go on," I said again, waving smoke away from my face.

"Okay, you ready for this? The investment company that took your money is called Adams Securities. They appear to be only a semi-legitimate

187

firm."

"What do you mean by that?"

"I say 'semi-legitimate' because, while they're licensed to do that kind of business, they hardly ever do any. They began operations exactly three days before Sullivan opened the account."

"Where you going with this?"

He smiled. "Right up Whitney's ass."

He finished off his coffee.

Then he said, "So I call Tallahassee. The Florida Department of Business and Professional Regulation. They look into Adams Securities. It's a hundred percent owned by a company called WA Financial Group."

"So what?"

"So this. WA Financial Group is a dummy corporation. It doesn't do anything except serve as a buffer between Adams Securities and the real owner."

"The real owner?"

"The real owner, the owner of WA Financial Group, and therefore of Adams Securities, is none other than Whitney-Adams Enterprises, Incorporated, a holding company which also happens to own all of Whitney's other businesses. Adams, it turns out, was his first wife's maiden name. She must've been some great pussy, huh?"

"What happened to the four hundred Gs?"

"Until just recently, nothing special. It went into a larger fund and from there into a few commercial real estate buys, strictly routine, and Sullivan even saw a little income from it. Then, about a month before you got out, Adams Securities pulled a little high-finance sleight-of-hand with debt-shifting and shell companies and a few other tricks. When the smoke cleared, the money was gone."

"Gone right into Whitney's pocket," I said.

"No doubt."

With a slightly flamboyant arm motion, Ryder crushed out his cigarette, signaling that the curtain had fallen.

I got up from the table.

"Thanks for the data."

"Hey, wait a second. I go to a shitload of trouble and that's all I get? Just a quick thanks?"

I kept walking toward the door, but turned back to say, "No. You also get the check. And my thanks for the coffee."

TWENTY-FOUR

Yale Lando told me my ID would be ready on the twelfth, which was tomorrow. But I thought I'd drop by just in case he got it together early.

First, though, I had to eat; I was starved. After leaving the Waffle House, I made sure I wasn't being tailed, then went down to a little spot on White Street, one of the DeLima joints, for a leisurely Cuban breakfast.

Around nine o'clock, I caught Yale outside his gate, just as he was hurrying into his house.

"Yo, Yale!" I hollered from my car.

He turned around and saw me.

"Hey, man! Come on in!" He rushed up to unlock his door.

"C'mere, Yale!"

He ignored me as he ran inside. I climbed out of Norma's Toyota and followed him through the gate, up the steps, into the house.

His house was nice and cool, providing refuge from the intensity of the sun. I relaxed immediately while he frantically flipped on the TV. After a couple of channel changes, he located his target.

A guy with white hair talking to another guy across a table.

"This is Phil Donahue. Y'ever see this show?"

I shook my head.

"This guy's great. He has all these guests on, you know, where they talk about current events and big issues and shit. Really interesting. He gets these people to open up to him and then, *bum*, he nails 'em."

After that little dramatic explanation, I thought he was ready to get down to business.

But instead, "Oh, and the audience! He even lets the audience ask questions. And people can phone in from home and ask questions. It's really great. I tried phoning in a couple of times, but I could never get through. Sometimes it's more lighthearted, but usually it's heavy shit like this. Events. And issues."

I took a seat on his dilapidated couch. We watched the show for a few minutes while Donahue held up a book which the other guy had apparently written. Donahue did most of the talking.

Then, as they broke for a commercial, Yale said, "I'll

bet I know why you're here."

"You got something for me?"

"You're in luck, Don Roy. It's all ready to go."

He went into the other room, the one where only he is allowed to go, and came out with a small envelope.

He sat next to me on the couch and peered inside the envelope. This was all for maximum effect, of course, his own little drama played out for my benefit. I half expected to see a glittering light flow out of the envelope and illuminate his face.

Finally, he took out three items.

"Here's your passport."

I checked it out as he carefully placed it in my hand. It looked fantastic, with its thick blue cover and the number punched out across the top. All perfectly legal, just like he'd told me. I flipped through it. It looked just like the real thing, with my photo stamped into it under the name of Roy Davis.

He handed me another item.

"Driver's license."

I studied it closely because a driver's license was more likely to be handled than a passport.

He was about to explain something to me when his head snapped back toward the TV.

Donahue raised his voice to his guest. They were arguing. From the audience's rowdy mood, they were clearly on Donahue's side, applauding everything he said.

"*Yes, Phil!*" cried Yale. "Don't take any shit from that right-wing motherfucker!"

He turned to face me, but only halfway, so he could still catch the action on the TV.

"You hear this? This fucking guy doesn't want the Brady Bill to go through. Shit, even Reagan is behind it! What fucking century is this guy living in, anyway? *Let him have it, Phil!*"

Thankfully, they went to another commercial.

Yale calmed down, then returned his attention to the driver's license. He pointed to the long number printed on it.

"This's where so many fakes fall apart," he said. "Each one of those figures means something, something the authorities use to tell if it's the real thing. For instance, the letter D right there at the beginning of the number. That's the first initial of the last name: Davis. If a cop sees that and it doesn't match up, you're toast."

He pulled out the last item.

"And here's your plastic."

He laid it on the coffee table. A Visa card, under the name of Charles Brockaway, complete with expiration date and everything.

I looked on the back. The signature area was blank.

Yale said, "Don't sign it right away. Practice the signature a few times so you can get comfortable with it, so it'll look natural. That way, it'll be easier to match it when you sign for a purchase."

I nodded.

"I can pick up the second card on the twenty-fifth? That right?"

"Check. Now, there's the minor matter of the money."

He returned his attention to the TV while I counted out twenty-one hundred dollars. As I gave it to him, he put it in the pocket of his cutoffs without counting it. Donahue and the other guy were getting into it again.

I patted Yale on the shoulder and left.

TWENTY-FIVE

I went to a pay phone to call Norma at her mother's up on Big Coppitt.

I told her I was on my way up there, then asked how would she like to run up to Miami. She thought it was a swell idea. So did I. Now that I was running plastic, I needed to buy some new clothes, but I didn't want to chance any buys in Key West.

Like Yale said, it's a small town.

Anyway, I'd been wearing the same three pairs of pants and a couple of shirts and guayaberas since I'd gotten out. I was tired of doing all that washing every two or three days, so I picked her up and we headed up the Keys for the mainland.

We got up there around mid-afternoon. She picked out a shopping mall, so we went in, looking for a couple of clothing stores.

I bought a bunch of stuff, including a few nice

things. I'd never had many nice clothes — I really was never too interested in them, you know? — but Norma insisted. I figured if she wanted me to look nice, then why shouldn't I?

I wanted to return the favor so we went to a women's store, so she could go crazy. She'd had even less her whole life than I ever did, and I really wanted to make things right for her.

If we were going to have a life together, then I figured I ought to do what I could for her, while I could do it.

It was beginning to dawn on me that the square life was just around the corner. I mean, I couldn't live on the con forever, not if I wanted to be with Norma. She was a wonderful woman, everything I ever hoped to have.

I owed her that much.

To get on the straight road.

Besides, there wasn't much action in Key West, anyway. That's why I'd left for Vegas before. So how long would it be this time before I'd run out of scams again?

No, Key West was...well...it was our home. So if Norma was willing to take a chance on me, then I didn't want her worrying every day of her life about whether or not I was going to prison.

Especially with the likes of Ortega out there, just itching to nail me for one thing or another.

We had a nice dinner that night in a cute little place on the ocean over in Miami Beach. Nothing real fancy, but we did get a bottle of wine.

Neither of us had ever done that before and it felt kind of strange. You know, where the guy brings the bottle out and pours a little and all that ceremonial shit. We really didn't know what to do, but the guy helped us with it, so it worked out okay.

It was a pretty nice little evening, and we both agreed we'd do it again sometime.

Afterward, we went to a hotel to spend the night, and what a night it was!

TWENTY-SIX

We stayed up in Miami another day, heading back on Saturday, the thirteenth.

I dropped Norma off at her mother's trailer, reminding both of them not to answer the door for anyone until I gave the all-clear. Norma's mother had moved to Big Coppitt Key a month or so ago, after having lived on Stock Island her whole life, so I was pretty sure no one knew where she was.

But with Vasiliev after her, I couldn't get overconfident.

Back in my room, I gathered up my piece and the muffler, along with a couple of extra clips, which I'd bought at a real gun shop up in Miami. Then I got into the car for a quick trip across the island to the Ocean Walk apartments.

There it was, in the parking lot right by the stairwell to Norma's building, the dark blue Land

Rover I'd seen the other day. I circled around the building, parked on the other side, then got out and made my way back around on foot, approaching it from behind.

As I crept closer to the Land Rover, I saw there was no one sitting inside. I glimpsed the plates. Broward County.

I went into the building, taking the back stairs up to Norma's floor. When I got to her apartment, I gently put my ear to her door. I heard the TV going.

I stayed still for a few minutes. Eventually, I heard voices in the room, speaking in a foreign language. I slowly attached the silencer to the end of my automatic. Then I made a fist and pounded on the door a couple of times.

The TV stopped immediately. After a little rapid talk in their language, one of them soon stood on the other side of the door.

"Who is it?" he asked in accented English.

I stood to one side of the door with my gun in one hand, the other hand covering the peephole.

"Police officers!" I said in my best cop voice. "Open up!"

After a moment's pause, in which he apparently tried to look through the peephole, he said, "I can't see you through little hole in door."

"Open up! Police! Open up *now!*"

"What do you want? Get away from hole!"

Then I said in a lower voice, but so he could still hear me, "Twenty-one-fifty to headquarters. Officers need assistance. Ocean Walk apartments, building—"

"Okay, okay!" he shouted. "You don't need more cops! I open up."

And he unbolted the door, but didn't unchain it. When he inched it open to peek through, I came bursting through it with all of my weight, breaking the chain and sending him reeling against the far wall. The revolver fell from his hand on impact.

His pal came running in from the living room, gun in hand, but I fired first. Two quiet pops found the mark, as he collapsed to the floor with small red stains across the center of his white shirt.

The guy who answered the door was still down, but recovered now. He reached for his piece on the floor. I put a heavy foot on his hand before he could get to it.

With the business end of my silencer touching his temple, I said, "What's your name, friend?"

"Alexei. Please, *ay-yy-y!* Please move foot!"

"Yeah, in a minute. But first, Alexei, what's this all about?

I ground my heel into the back of his hand. I felt

one of the little bones crack. He yelped.

"I said, what's this all about?"

He gasped and groaned. I pushed the silencer harder against his head.

"It's gonna get a lot worse if you don't tell me right now."

"Is Whitney! Whitney and Yuri!" he said through his gasps. "Is all I know! I do what Yuri tells me! Is all I know!"

"Where's Yuri? Where is he?"

"He fly back to Lauderdale the other day. He have business."

"When's he coming back?"

I stepped a little harder on his broken hand, sending major hurt all through his body.

"He — *oh-hh* — he come back tomorrow! Please! Move foot! *Please!*"

I gave one more full-weight heel-grind into his hand, breaking another bone or two.

He screamed, then I let up.

As I bent down to pick up his gun, he groaned again while he tenderly cradled his injured hand, glad for the relief.

I pulled him to his feet, then made him help me clean up the blood from the floor by his buddy's corpse. We wrapped the body in Norma's bedspread before carrying it downstairs.

Once we got to the ground floor, I fished through his pockets, finding the Land Rover key. The Rover wasn't far away, but I went and got it. As soon as I brought it over by the stairwell, we loaded the body inside.

I grabbed Alexei by his collar. With all the upper body force I could muster, I shoved him up against the side of the car.

"You tell Yuri to leave my woman alone," I snarled, "or he's gonna wish he died as easily as your friend here. You understand me, Alexei?"

He moved his head up and down, fear all over his face.

"If Yuri wants me, I'll be around. But I mean it, if he fucks with my woman, I'll make him eat his own balls! You got it?"

I pushed him away without waiting for an answer, then headed back to my car.

SETUP ON FRONT STREET

TWENTY-SEVEN

Doctor Chicago stepped off the plane three days later, on the sixteenth.

I had to admit, he was looking good. The years seemed a lot kinder to him than they were to me. Of course, his work leaned toward the high-volume end of things, so it netted him a lot more dough than mine ever got me. Plus, he never got caught.

"Hey, hey!" he cried as he came to me with open arms. "My man! Don Roy! So great to see you again!"

His slender arms hugged my big shoulders as best they could, and I returned the embrace.

"Same old Doc!" I said, pulling away for a good look at him. "You don't look a day older, man."

It was true. He had to be in his late fifties, but his eyes were dark and clear, his big smile showed gleaming teeth, and his skin was still smooth, as if freshly-coated with a fine, dark polish.

We threw some of that small talk back and forth for a few seconds. The tight little airport terminal building had no air conditioning, so it got pretty thick in there.

"You got any bags?" I asked.

"Right here."

He held up a carry-on suitcase, along with what appeared to be an empty satchel. "Everything the doctor ordered."

"Let's go." We headed for the car.

On the way back from the airport, I took a detour to Key Haven to make a run past Whitney's house.

"There it is," I said, slowing down to give him a good look.

Disbelief came out of his eyes and his voice.

"That's it?"

He gazed hard at it as I drove by.

"That's it? No gates? No walls?"

"That's it."

"You mean, it's just some bullshit hundred-dollar dinger inside the door? Which probably has a two-dollar deadbolt on it?"

"That's it," I repeated.

"How 'bout animals? Any dogs? Or any pets at all likely to make a noise?"

"No."

"Man, I don't get it. You could do this yourself with

your eyes closed. What you need me for?"

"You know I don't do a lot of this kind of work, Doc. Besides, this is a big deal to me. I need the best. That's why I called you. I need those files, and he can't know he's been broken into. I'll make copies of the ones I need, and then you'll have to return them, okay?"

He nodded.

"The owner? He gone now?"

"Left this morning for three days. I think only the live-in maid is there."

"Shi-it!" he grumbled. "I could take that place while she was in the other room eatin' breakfast."

I turned the car around to drive by once more on our way out of the neighborhood.

"Like I told you, man. You done a lot for me. You'll get your files, no-o-o problem."

***

That night, Doc made his preparations in my room. He put on his all-black throwaway over his regular street clothes, assembled a few pieces of high and lowe-tech equipment into an oversized fanny pack, and wrapped the whole package around his lean waist. Finally, he grabbed the empty satchel to put the files in.

I'd drawn him a layout of the house, pinpointing

the file cabinet's location. Then I drove him out to Key Haven just before 3:30 AM. The streets all around were empty and silent. All the houses were dark.

"Let me off right in front," he said as we approached Whitney's house. "Drive around for fifteen minutes. Got it? Fifteen minutes." I nodded. He added, "Come back and pass by the house. You won't see me. I'll be in the bushes. When you come by, I'll make for the car and get in the driver's side back door. Leave it ajar so I don't make no noise opening it. Got it?"

"Got it."

"If you don't see me runnin' for the car, drive around the block and keep doin' it till you see me. Okay?"

I said okay, and we synched our watches. After he got out, I watched him creep onto Whitney's front lawn.

Within seconds, he disappeared into the dark.

Exactly fifteen minutes later, I returned. I motored down the deserted street, slowing way down to look for Doc.

Suddenly, he was at the back door and in the car, almost as though he'd just popped out of the pavement. We exited the neighborhood while he peeled off his black clothing.

"Piece o' fuckin' cake, man! What'd I tell you!" He

patted the satchel. "You got you some files, my man!"

I half-turned around to face him. I was still driving.

"Everything go all right? No problems?"

"None whatsoever. The locks, the dinger, they all went down without a hitch. Man, I was in and out in eleven minutes. My biggest problem was waitin' in the bushes till you came back." He hefted the satchel. "Not many files in there, though. I was expecting a ton of 'em, but there's only a few. Hope you get what you're lookin' for."

***

Back in my room, we had a couple of beers to celebrate.

I looked through the files. Most of them concerned Adams Securities and its ownership by WA Financial Group. There was a copy of the agreement between Adams and Sully for the four hundred large, just like Ryder had said. But mostly, it just looked like a lot of legalese bullshit.

Until I came across one document that stood out.

It appeared to be the purchase of a building on Duval Street--the building which housed Sullivan's Irish Pub. The buyer was none other than WA Properties, a subsidiary of WA Financial Group, and the broker of record was listed as Adams Realty, Inc, a division of Adams Securities.

The deal was dated May 4, 1989, one day after Sully gave Adams our dough. A copy of Sully's lease with the previous owner was attached.

Then there was one file marked "WA-Caribbean Holdings". I opened it and read it with great interest.

WA-Caribbean Holdings was the name of a company, owned by none other than Whitney-Adams Enterprises. From what I could make out, WA-Caribbean Holdings itself owned a bunch of smaller companies.

One was called Trans-Caribbean Airways, a small airline which, according to the documents, appeared to have the inside track on the Key West-to-Havana route when the big day came.

Another was Cuba-Caribe, Inc., which a memo said would be licensed "at some future date" by the Cuban government to build a hotel/casino in downtown Havana, plus one on the beach at Varadero. The officers of Cuba-Caribe, Inc. all had Russian names, except for the company president, one Wilson J Whitney, Junior. The one and only BK himself.

I got out Ryder's phone number and called him right away.

"Good morning!" I said with all the perkiness I

could muster. "This's Doyle. Did you sleep well?"

He tried to speak. I think he said something like, "What time is it?"

"It's quarter of five! Rise and shine! The new day is here. Come on, the FBI never sleeps, right?"

After a few seconds, he became conscious, cursed me a little, then finally spoke clearly.

"All right, what is it? And this better be good."

"Put on your best regulation Hawaiian shirt and meet me at the Waffle House in a half an hour. I've got something you'll want to see."

TWENTY-EIGHT

This time I waited for him.

I had the files in a Sears bag next to me on the seat. It took him nearly an hour to get there from the time of the phone call, but what the hell. He works for the government.

You have to expect that.

He quickly poured himself a cup of coffee. The aroma alone seemed to soothe him. Then, he lit a cigarette with his blowtorch, blew on his coffee to cool it down, and planted that cellular telephone perfectly in the center of the table. This guy was all ritual.

Finally, he was got down to business.

"Let's have it," he said.

I showed him the files, all but the one on WA-Caribbean Holdings. He examined them pretty closely. Whitney's contract to buy the building, along with Sully's accompanying lease, stopped him in his tracks, as it had me. He read it carefully.

"Here it is," he said, pointing to a date on the lease document. "Sullivan's lease was for ten years, and it was set to expire on July 1, 1991. Just a couple of weeks from now. *And* he had the option of renewing it for another ten."

"So what? Isn't that pretty routine?"

"Wait. In addition, according to the sale document, the lease agreement with Sullivan was binding on Whitney when he bought the building because Sullivan had already been occupying the premises for around eight years or so. Now, if you read this clause here—" He pointed to the middle of a long paragraph containing mostly impenetrable lingo. "It says if Sullivan wanted to renew the lease, which he hadn't done yet, he had to exercise his option no later than ninety days before the expiration date."

He spoke as if that one fact wrapped the whole thing up.

"April first," I said. "So what."

"Sullivan was killed during the early morning hours of April first."

I ran it over in my mind so it would all fall into place.

We pull the job out in Vegas, I go down for it and do a three-year bit. Sully keeps the money and, as he told me that night when I shook him down, he'd washed it through the club.

Washing four hundred dimes through a bar takes time. It can't all show up in just one or two nights. So he's patient, doing it very carefully, spreading it out over a year.

So when it's all nice and clean, he turns it over to Adams Securities. That would be in May of eighty-nine. They probably came to him, since Whitney most likely knew Sully had a lot of cash on his hands.

The very next day, Whitney buys the building that Sully's bar is in. But Sully doesn't know that Whitney and Adams are one and the same.

Anyway, Adams takes the money and invests it, just like Sully had said. For a couple of years, they show him a little income from it—standard procedure for a long con. So of course, he thinks everything's aces.

But then, about a month or two ago, things change.

The money suddenly disappears behind Whitney's smoke and mirrors, and Sully freaks out. Now we're coming up on April 1, the drop-dead date for Sully to renew his lease. The bar's doing great, he's making a pile of dough, he's even thinking about expanding into Cuba, just like he told me that night in his office. No reason to think he wouldn't renew for another ten years.

Then, I happen to come back to town.

Of course, there was no way he could give me my share of the take, much less tell me he'd been stung for the whole load. He knew I'd think he was holding out on me.

And he was right. I would've.

So I push him around a little, and a few nights later he's lying in the street with his throat cut—the very night before he's scheduled to renew his lease.

Word gets out that I threatened him, and presto!

The perfect frame.

I chewed on all of this for a minute. Then I took it around the block for Ryder, who was crushing out his cigarette.

"It fits," he said. "But wait. There's more."

"Go."

"While I'm on the phone to the office in Tallahassee, it occurs to me that they're the people who also issue liquor licenses. I inquire about the Sullivan's Irish Pub building, and guess what?"

"What?"

"On April third, a mere two days after Sullivan was killed, they receive an application for a liquor license to be used at that address. The application stated the owner of the building, WA Properties, was leasing it out to a company called Keys Good Times, Inc., for the purpose of converting it into a strip joint."

"A strip joint?"

"Right. The kind of place where you can launder money in great quantities and no one knows the difference. What's more, the officers of Keys Good Times, Inc., the actual applicants for the liquor license, were two gentlemen with Russian names. I ran them through our files. They're clean, but you can be sure they're fronts for the Russian mob."

"So Whitney must've promised the building to the Russians for their strip joint, figuring they could wash money a lot quicker than they could through a regular bar. Is that right?"

Ryder said yes, that's right.

I kept going. It fell into place for me literally as I spoke.

"Whitney probably warned Sully, maybe through BK, to let the lease expire. Sully wasn't the type of guy you could push around, so he probably told BK to shove it. Whitney couldn't afford to alienate the Russians, since they had their hearts set on his building, so Sully had to go."

"You're catching on. However, there's no real evidence that Whitney's done anything illegal."

He pulled out another cigarette, then tamped it, filter end down, on the tabletop.

I said, "But listen to this. The night I braced Sully for the money, he mentioned a deal he had working with BK. He said he was going to open up a place in Cuba after Castro is gone. He must've somehow gotten wind of Whitney's Russian connection and their Cuban ambitions, and tried to bite off a little piece for himself."

I pulled out the WA-Caribbean Holdings file.

"And check this out. A paper trail leading from Whitney to the Russians, then straight to Cuba."

Ryder pored over the documents through widening eyes. He got what he wanted.

I looked at my watch. Ten till seven. Outside, up in the black sky, the first traces of dawn were slowly seeping in from the east. I needed to sleep.

"You want copies of these files?" I asked him.

"Naturally."

"Make what you need," I told him. "But get them back to me by this afternoon."

I left the Waffle House and drove back to my room. Doc was still asleep on the couch. I tried to be quiet as I got out of my clothes, then crawled into bed.

Sleep hit me right away.

TWENTY-NINE

I got the files back from Ryder later that day. That night, Doc returned them to Whitney's cabinet with no trouble. He even made sure they were in alphabetical order when he put them back.

Ever since Doc got in town, I could tell he knew this was no ordinary job. He knew better than to come right out and ask if I was in a jam, but he hinted around at it.

So the following morning, I sat him down over coffee and told him what I wanted to do.

"So you see, Doc, things could get messy."

"Shi-it, messy don't bother me, man. Besides, from what you just told me, you might need me in there. Count me in."

"Sorry, man. You're not the violent type. If any shit goes down, I don't want you getting hurt."

"Hurt, shit! You don't hafta worry 'bout me. I can

take care of myself. And I'll be watchin' your back while I'm at it."

I had half a mind to take him to the airport right then.

Except that he was right when he said I might need him.

"Okay, but bring the satchel. And you stay out of the way until I need you. If I need you at all. Agreed?"

He flashed his big, toothy smile.

***

I knew I'd need a driver, too. So early that evening, Doc and I went to Mambo's.

There were only about six or seven guys in there, and the baseball game on the TV had the attention of most of them. The jukebox, normally pumping with hot-blooded Cuban rhythms, sat silent. The irresistible aroma of Cuban food sprawled out over the whole joint.

Shimmy circled the pool table, chalking his cue, in search of the ideal shot. I steered Doc to my booth, then went right to the pay phone.

She answered on the second ring.

"Rita. It's Don Roy."

"Why, hello, sweetheart. Got something for a lonely

girl?"

She sounded like she really meant it. I have to admit, I'd been thinking about her a little since our last meeting. Not that I'd ever act on it—I'm not that idiotic, and besides, I've got Norma.

But I did think about it.

"Actually, you can do something for me. Can I come over? Preferably when BK's not around."

As soon as I said that, I realized what it sounded like.

She took the cue. "Well, lover, you know you can come over anytime when he's not here. I'm having workmen in and around the house all day tomorrow...we're doing some remodeling. But his father's coming back from the Bahamas tomorrow night and he and some other guys are picking the old buzzard up at the airport at eight-thirty."

"Some other guys?"

I didn't like that end of it.

"Yeah. He didn't say who, but he said they all had business to discuss out at Key Haven." She began to coo rather than speak. "He prob'ly won't be back till ten-thirty or eleven."

Someone fed the jukebox and a lively merengue tune jumped out of it. Punchy trumpets and percussion got through to the baseball crowd at the bar. They started drumming their fingers, swaying on the barstools. I looked over at Doc. Even he felt the feverish rhythms, bobbing his head up and down.

"Rita, it's not what you're thinking. I just need to talk to you is all."

"Sometimes talking's a turn-on, too, you know."

She made me smile, but I had to get past it.

"I'm gonna need a big favor from you. And I can't ask you over the phone. I'd rather ask you in person. At your house."

Her voice turned pouty. "Okay, be that way. Eight o'clock. You know where we live?"

"That big house on William Street, right?"

"Right. See you tomorrow."

I tapped Shimmy on the shoulder, beckoning him over to my booth. As soon as we sat down, I ordered beers all around.

"Hey, Don Roy," he said. "What's up?"

"Shimmy, this's Doctor Chicago. I think I told you about him. Class A crib man from Vegas."

"Pleasure," Shimmy said, shaking Doc's hand.

The waiter brought the beers. We each took that first frosty sip from the new brown bottle.

I turned back to Shimmy.

"You still remember how to drive?"

He chuckled under his breath.

219

"What've you got?"

"It's local. We go tomorrow night. It pays a dime. You just drive us to the location and back. You wait in the car. It's just a house, so there shouldn't be any rough stuff, but if there is, I'll make it two dimes. Bring your piece, just in case. And tight rubber gloves for all of us."

He threw a glance at Doc.

"Crib man?" He looked back at me. "We doing a B and E?"

"Not really. There's a safe where we're going. Doc comes into the picture just in case we need him to open it."

That seemed to meet with his approval.

"What time you want me?"

"Be ready to go at seven-thirty."

***

Doc and I showed up at Mambo's at seven-fifteen the next evening. We hadn't eaten since lunch. Doc was decked in his black throwaways. Shimmy was already there, waiting for us.

We all sat down in my booth, then ordered coffee. A little small talk here and there, and pretty soon it was seven-thirty.

"Where're you parked?" I asked Shimmy.

"Around the corner."

We all got up and left.

Shimmy's car was a tan '77 Buick Electra 225, or deuce-and-a-quarter, as he called it.

It looked exactly like your basic clunky old piece of shit from the seventies, but he'd dropped a 455-cubic-inch Buick engine under the hood, so that after a couple of minor modifications, he was getting almost four hundred horsepower. It could do a hundred and fifty with no problem, outrunning even the cops.

I rode shotgun, Doc slid into the back.

"William Street," I said. "The Whitney house."

Shimmy raised his eyebrows and whistled through his teeth.

"Man, BK lives there now. What's the shot?"

"Just drive. I'll explain when we get there."

The house was less than a mile from Mambo's. We got there at around twenty-five to eight. I had Shimmy circle the block, then park in a metered spot with the engine off.

The house, a big white Victorian thing, loomed about half a block in front of us on the other side of the street. A white picket fence ran down the front of the property along the sidewalk. Four big coconut palms, just inside the fence, stretched up toward the high, thin clouds that drifted in from the south. Industrial-strength floodlights positioned at the base of the palms pointed at the house, lighting up everything in sight.

From where we sat, we had a good view. I spotted BK's Dodge in the driveway.

I turned to face the two of them.

"Okay, we're gonna wait here a little while. Pretty soon, someone, maybe the Russians, are gonna pick BK up. Then they're going to the airport to meet the old man, who's coming back from the Bahamas. Not long after that, I'm going in. Rita's there and she'll let me in. I want what's in their safe. If I can't get into it for some reason, I'm gonna—Shimmy, where's your flashlight?"

He reached under the driver's seat and put a mag light in my hand.

"I'm gonna go to the window and shine this flashlight at the car. I'll blink it twice. If you see that, Doc, that's your cue. Come on in, and bring the satchel."

Doc nodded. Then I said to Shimmy, "You stay here the whole time. As soon as I get inside the house, start the engine and keep it running. This'll probably go off without a hitch, but keep your eyes peeled anyway. If BK and the Russians come back for some reason while we're still in there, get your heater out and come running. Doc's not holding, so I may need all the firepower help I can get."

He reached behind him, pulling a large automatic from his rear waistband. I made it to be a nine millimeter.

He jacked it, then said firmly, "I'll be there, bubba."

THIRTY

Around five till eight, the dark blue Land Rover cruised by, drawing up in front of the house.

As best I could make out, it held three men. I couldn't tell if one of them was Yuri Vasiliev, but the one riding shotgun was older, maybe in his fifties or sixties.

Right behind was Whitney's silver Mercedes. From the long hair of the two occupants, I made them to be Milton and Bradley.

The Mercedes honked twice. Within twenty seconds, BK ambled out of the house carrying a briefcase. Rita closed the door behind him. He ducked into the Mercedes. I caught her briefly scanning the street to see if I'd arrived.

The cars drove away in the general direction of the airport, then I said, "We'll give them a few minutes to make sure they don't come back for anything."

Five minutes went by. I glanced at Doc and Shimmy before getting out of the car. Their faces told me they were ready.

In less than a minute, I stood at the door of the house. I was uneasy under all that light; shit, it was like daylight up there.

Fortunately, the door opened before I had a chance to knock.

"I knew you were out there somewhere, lurking around in the shadows," she said.

I quickly moved inside the house.

There in the hallway, out of the floodlit entrance, I adjusted my eyes for a second. Then I got a full look at her. Her white cotton blouse fit her just right, showing off her stuff just as she'd planned, with skin-tight pants that begged to be removed. Her come-on smile fronted all of it.

Even in the dim hall light, she glistened.

As I checked her out, I said, "Just your average hanging-around-the-house outfit?"

She shrugged.

"What's a girl to do? Especially when she's looking for excitement."

I ignored her play.

"Rita, there's something I've got to see. It's important."

She reached for the top button on her blouse. I pulled her hand away.

"No, come on, now. This is serious."

"Oh, all right," she groused. "What is it?"

"I need to see the contents of your safe."

That brought her down to earth, and fast.

"The safe? What on earth for?"

"I just need to look in it."

"Well, Don Roy, I don't know..."

I took her hand in mine.

"Rita, you told me the old man keeps things in there.

"Right," she said. "So?"

"So...I need to see what he's got. You said he keeps it separate from BK's and your stuff. Like in a different cubbyhole or something."

"Well, yes. He does."

"I need to see it. Now."

She paused. She was looking at me, but right through me, you know what I mean? In her mind, she was rationalizing it, working it all out--how the old man had treated her like shit, how BK had jacked her around, how things hadn't worked out quite the way...

"Come on," she said. "It's upstairs."

Her spiked heels clicked as she led me across the tile floor.

SETUP ON FRONT STREET

We went up the staircase, which wasn't nearly as grand as the rest of the house. There was some artwork on the wall going up the steps, but I couldn't tell what it was, whether or not it was any good.

At the top, we went into the first bedroom.

It was obviously their bedroom. Or at least hers, whenever she banished BK to another room, which I figured was probably pretty often these days. They had all the routine stuff in there. King-sized bed, some kind of makeup table with a fancy mirror, a couple of dressers, along with a huge closet in the corner.

She led me to the closet and it sucked my breath right out of me.

It was bigger than my room, I swear! This thing was about twenty feet deep. I stood in the doorway and I saw clothes, all hers, lining the walls. Along a section of one of the walls was a wide, pigeonhole-type structure just for her shoes. She must've had a hundred pairs.

Un-fucking-believable.

She moved a suitcase out of the way back in the far left-hand corner. Reaching down to where the baseboards met, she grabbed the thick carpeting with her thumb and index finger, then peeled it back. It had already been cut into a two-foot by two-foot square, so that piece just lifted up off the floor.

227

Beneath it was the door of the safe.

"Don Roy, I...I..."

Her eyes pleaded with me to call the whole thing off.

"Come on, girl. Don't quit on me now. Not when we're this close."

She spun the combination dial a few times, stopping carefully on the right numbers, then gave the handle a turn. It clicked.

She swung the door open, resting it against the rear wall of the closet. She edged back as though she were afraid of what was inside.

I moved closer, holding Shimmy's flashlight. Inside I could see the safe was divided into two equal compartments.

Each one had a small, cheap door about six or eight inches square.

Each one opened with a key.

"Which one's the old man's?" I asked her. She pointed to the one on the left and I said, "You got the key?"

"No. He keeps it."

I headed over to the window. It faced the back yard. I went across the hall to what looked like a guest bedroom.

At the window in that room, I slid the curtain back

a little bit. Beyond the house's blinding security lights below was William Street. I could barely make out the car down the street a little way through the harsh glare. I blinked the flashlight twice, hoping they'd see it. No one moved from the car, so I blinked twice more.

Finally, I saw the car's back door open a little. I knew it was wide enough for Doc.

"What are you doing?" Rita asked.

"Making sure I get inside that compartment."

I went downstairs and let him in.

He followed me upstairs without a word, without a sound. I had to turn around at the top of the stairs to make sure he was still there.

"Where is it?" he asked.

"In here."

I brought him into the closet. He took the flashlight from my hand, aiming its powerful beam at the safe's interior.

"It's the compartment on the left," I offered.

"How'd you open the safe?"

"Rita knew the combination."

"Shi-it," he hissed. "This's one of those low-grade jobs. I coulda opened it in prob'ly half the time."

After one quick look, he set the satchel on the floor, reaching into his fanny pack. He gently pulled out a slim leatherette box and laid it on the floor in front of him.

Inside, carefully arranged on a bed of velvet, lay a variety of lock picks—long, pointy devices of different widths and gauges. He selected two, then inserted them into the lock on the left. A couple of turns later, I saw him pull the picks out, opening the door in the process.

"There you go," he said proudly as he moved to one side.

He handed me the flashlight. I trained it on Whitney's sanctuary. There was some cash, but not much else. I reached in and took it out. It consisted of two banded wads of hundred dollar bills. I made each one to be about ten large.

"God *damn!*" Rita said. "I had no fucking idea..."

I laughed. "This's just pocket change. Something he can walk around with. If he needs a little dough and he doesn't want to drive all the way out to Key Haven, where he no doubt keeps the serious money, he can just drop in here and pick up a little loose change."

I lifted the money out of its hiding place and into my pants pocket.

We went back downstairs. I pulled a scrap of paper out of my wallet and, using BK's desk phone, I dialed the number that was scribbled down.

"Ryder," I said when he answered. "In about thirty

minutes, Whitney will be landing at the airport. His two goons, along with BK and the Russians, will be there to greet him. You can nab them all at once. I'm going out to his Key Haven house right now to get something out of his safe that belongs to me. You might want to come out there later on. I'll leave the safe open for you. Maybe there'll be something interesting inside it."

I hung up and turned to Rita.

"Now, where does the old man keep his other safe out in the Key Haven house?"

"Same place as here. Corner of the big closet, under the carpeting."

"Come on, Doc," I said. "We're going to Key Haven."

THIRTY-ONE

Shimmy expertly maneuvered the big deuce through the narrow streets of the city, then finally out to Key Haven. On the way out there, I laid it out for him and Doc, including the Whitney-Russian connection.

I emphasized that the Russians were the baddest of the badasses, but if everything went according to plan, we should be out of Key Haven altogether by the time they got back from the airport.

"Any way you cut it," I said to them, "this is really my affair. There *is* a risk, and you guys don't have to chance it."

"That BK's an A-1 asshole," Shimmy said. "I've never liked him or any of those Whitneys. They've ruined this island. Anything I can do to fuck them up, I'm in."

I looked at Doc. He couldn't wait to weigh in.

SETUP ON FRONT STREET

"Hey, man, you know I got to be in. You cats couldn't get in that house without me, not even if you had the keys."

I smiled, mostly inside.

"Okay. We're going to go in and crack Whitney's safe. If we get what I think is in there, you're both getting a fat bonus. And I mean fat."

***

The other night, when Doc and I were out here, the whole street was deserted. No lights, no activity, no nothing. Just your typical slumbering suburb with everybody tucked away in their nice, secure beds.

Tonight it looked like the crossroads of the fucking world.

Traffic everywhere, cars parked all up and down both sides of the street, as well as on the side streets, too. Those cars that were moving were jostling for parking spots, but not finding many. They were mostly high-end jobs — Caddies, Mercedes, Jags, that kind of thing. We saw lots of happy people walking from their cars, all in one direction.

Toward a gigantic house at the end of the street.

We rumbled past Whitney's place in the thick traffic. No cars were in the driveway. As we neared the big house at the end, we could see there was some kind of party going on.

Tall, wrought iron security gates opened into a wide, yawning welcome. Valets crammed all those ritzy cars next to one another at all angles, even dumping them into a couple of neighboring yards.

The place throbbed with music and people, and the grounds were all lit up. From the looks of things, this was the party of the year, one you wouldn't want to miss if you gave a shit about that kind of thing. I got to wondering if Whitney had been invited.

Shimmy attempted a U-turn into the heaviest traffic. After a minute or two of trying to bring the big car around, a couple of people started honking, but finally we were facing the way we came in. He slowed way down as we headed back, passing Whitney's house.

"What now?" he asked.

"Turn down there."

I pointed at a nearby side street and he made the turn.

It, too, was packed with cars, so we didn't find a spot until we'd turned another corner to go around the block. By now we'd gone nearly three blocks from Whitney's house, and we couldn't see it from here. We circled the block again, but there were no convenient spots to be had.

Just before coming back out onto Whitney's street, Shimmy stopped at the stop sign around the corner from his house and shrugged.

"Why don't we just park in the driveway?"

"Because if they come back and see a car in the driveway, their guns come out, and whoever's in the car won't stand a chance."

I told Doc to get the door to the house open for us. He slipped out, becoming one with the night as he crossed the street toward Whitney's lawn.

We drove around the block once more.

No luck.

Pausing again at the stop sign, we could see that both sides of the street were still lined with parked cars. The big V-8 idled on the corner, its full-throated hum hinting at its hidden power.

My eyes moved to Shimmy. The overhead street light cast a whitish film across the side of his face. The line of his jaw was tight and grim, and his clear eyes stared straight ahead. Beyond the windshield, all the coconut palms along the street waved in the warm evening breeze.

"You know," I said, "if they get back while we're still in there, there's going to be trouble, and it could be real bad. Two of the Russians will be holding for sure, probably Whitney's boys, too."

Shimmy remained silent, his gaze fixed on the windshield.

"We're probably gonna have to take out all four guns," I said softly.

"I know."

His eyes narrowed.

"If it comes to that, and they draw down on us, you take Whitney's two boys. They're the ones with the long hair. I'll do the Russians."

He turned toward me.

"I've got a sawed-off in the trunk. You want to use it? It'll do a lot more business than that popgun you're holding."

"Go ahead and get it."

He got out and went to the back, looked around to make sure no one was watching, and retrieved the shotgun. Easing the trunk shut, he got back in the car.

"Here it is. Modified Remington twelve-gauge."

I could tell by the way it sat in his grip that it was a well-balanced weapon. He started to give it to me. I pushed it back at him.

"You keep it. Let me use your automatic."

He pulled the pistol, then handed it my way, butt first, along with a couple of loaded magazines. I put one clip in each of the top pockets of my guayabera.

"Gloves?" I asked.

He produced two pair. We snapped them on.

He had about a dozen extra shells for the shotgun, which he loaded into his pockets.

"You know, Don Roy, I'm glad we're doing this. Like I said, I've always hated BK. Always trying to weasel out of paying Mambo on his sports bets whenever I went to collect. And then, what he did to Norma. Just to pay off his fucking debts! Now it's his turn to pay. And it's about goddamn time."

I put a hand on Shimmy's tense forearm.

"Let's not get ahead of ourselves, bubba. If it comes to that, we only take out the guns. BK's probably not gonna have one. Well...let me put it another way. If he finds one, okay, let him have it. But we're not murderers. We don't do that shit."

He ground his teeth together. As he paused to look down at the shells in his hand, he sent me a single reluctant nod.

Right then, my thoughts drifted to Norma.

I recalled the pledges I'd made to her, the bond between us, the life we'd have together when this was all over. I thought of walking with her, hand-in-hand, to...to meet our future, whatever the hell it was, to meet it head on.

All I needed was my share of the money, and I felt

we could pull it off. I really did.

The way it looked to me, as long as it was the two of us sticking together, we could face any goddamn thing the world threw down in front of us.

From out of nowhere: "You boys ready?"

It was Doc, back in the car. I had no idea how he'd gotten there.

I snapped out of my thoughts.

"What've we got?" I asked him.

"Same way I got in before. There's one of them doggie doors in the back. You know, a panel on the back door to the house that swings in and out to let the dog out whenever he wants. Judging from the size of it, I'd say it's a pretty big mutt, too."

I said to Doc, "I didn't think Whitney had a dog."

"He don't. At least, there wasn't one there on the two occasions I've visited him. My guess is it was prob'ly there from the last owner of the house."

"Doc," I said, "that's not gonna do me any good. I'm too big to get through one of those things."

"Yeah, I know. That's why I slipped through it myself and unlocked the kitchen door for you. All you apes got to do is just walk right in."

Shimmy and I both chuckled pretty good.

A minute later, a spot finally opened up on Whitney's side of the street, about fifty feet from his driveway. Shimmy moved the car over to it, muscling his way in, while pissing off some other sap in a Lexus who had his eye on it at the same time. The Lexus was a hair too late, so he backed away from Shimmy's aggressive maneuvering.

Before I got out of the car, I turned toward the back seat to look at Doc.

"The safe in here is similar to the one we just saw," I told him. "You open it up and then get the hell out of there. Come back out here and start the car. You're gonna have to be our substitute driver."

"No problem, man. I can handle it."

"Wait for us with the motor running. While we're inside, work the front wheels into a position where you can pull straight out of this parking spot. We won't close the doors all the way. If you see us running out of the house, get ready to move fast."

"I got it, man. You just make sure you get your white asses outta there in one piece, awright?"

I looked straight at him. "If the Land Rover and the Mercedes show up while we're inside...say a prayer."

Shimmy slid the pump on his shotgun, moving the first shell into the chamber. The deadly sound froze us for a moment, reminding all of us of what we were about to do.

As if on cue, Shimmy and I took a deep breath at

the same time. We got out of the car, pushing the doors almost closed.

Then we moved silently toward the back of the house.

THIRTY-TWO

The unlocked door awaited us.

We slipped inside, across the big, unlit kitchen and into the dining room. Beyond that was the main hallway.

The huge living room sat off to one side, with the office right next to it. The hallway led to Whitney's bedroom. Just like Rita said, in the corner of his closet was a piece of carpeting that lifted up to reveal the safe. Doc took a look at it.

"It's a different model than the other one," he said.

"Can you get inside?" I asked.

"Oh yeah. Just gonna take me a little bit longer, is all."

I looked at my watch. Eight-thirty.

Time for Whitney's plane to arrive. Give him a few minutes to wait for his bags, then no more than ten or twelve minutes out to Key Haven.

241

A little drop of sweat broke out of my hairline, beginning a slow roll down the side of my face. I let it go.

Shimmy stood guard outside the closet doorway. The darkened bedroom was illuminated only by the slender shaft of dim closet light, as well as whatever light could slink in from the street. Long shadows fell across his taut figure, clad in a black tank top and black pants. His twelve gauge was at the ready.

Doc fiddled a few minutes more with the safe, cursing it under his breath.

"Should we forget it?" I asked.

"Naw, naw, I'll get it."

Nervously, I glimpsed my watch again. Eight-thirty-six.

Then I heard a little click. The door to the safe jerked open.

"There you go," Doc said with a smile.

I looked inside. There were no closed compartments, only a ton of cash.

I turned to Doc. "Okay, man, scram. Get the car going. We'll take care of this. And leave the satchel."

Doc hustled through the hallway, out into the night while Shimmy and I loaded up the satchel with lots and lots of those 10K banded wads. Beneath the cash, there was a lot of paperwork, some of it in Russian.

I left it, while leaving the safe open, as well.

As we headed into the hallway, we were stopped cold by the sound of the front door opening. We ducked back into the bedroom.

They talked in low tones as they entered the house. Whitney's voice sailed above the others. From what I could tell, they were all here.

In a moment, their voices faded as they went into another room, probably the office.

We crept into the hallway toward the front of the house. As we neared the dining room, we realized we couldn't go back through it to the kitchen door without being seen by everyone in the office.

I thought about making a run for it, but it might well get us both shot in the back. Just a couple of low-class burglars who got what was coming to them. Whitney would probably get a medal.

I whispered to Shimmy, "Let's take them now."

He nodded, tightening his grip on his big weapon.

Whitney was talking, but when I stepped into the room, all heads jerked around in my direction. Shimmy moved in behind me.

I took a quick count.

Straight ahead, Whitney sat at the power desk in the corner, BK in one of the big leather chairs in front and a little to the left of it, and an older guy wearing a sportcoat in the other chair. Standing behind the chairs way over to the left were my old pal Alexei from Norma's place, and Yuri Vasiliev, looking even colder than his photo. Milton and Bradley sat on the sofa on the right by the far wall.

Everybody jerked around in our direction, stunned by the intrusion.

Alexei's hand instinctively moved toward his waistband.

"Don't even think about it, Alexei," I said, pointing the nine millimeter directly at his midsection.

"Now, everybody put your hands where we can see them."

Whitney stood up.

"What the hell is this, Doyle? What are you after?"

"Sit down!" I said. "BK. Get up and get all the guns in the room. Start with Alexei here."

The older Russian spoke.

"Wilson. Who is this...this *thug*?" he said in accented English.

"You'll never get away with this, Doyle," Whitney said. "You're a fucking dead man."

"You think about this," I told him. "You might get there before I do. BK, get moving!"

BK got up from his chair, easing over to a spot behind Alexei, reaching under the front of the Russian's tropical shirt.

"Slowly, BK," I warned him. "And use only your thumb and forefinger. Drop it on the floor."

He pulled Alexei's heater out and let it drop.

"Nice and easy. Kick it over to me," I said. He did, and then did the same with Yuri.

"All right, BK. Now Milton and Bradley."

He went over to the sofa. Bradley tried to stare me down.

"Easy, Bradley. Don't get any big ideas."

Once all the guns were in the center of the floor, I kicked them one by one underneath the big couch next to the end table that held the secret file cabinet.

I turned to Whitney.

"Now, Mr Whitney, somebody in this room is going to have to answer for Frankie Sullivan."

I tossed a glance at Vasiliev. He caught it.

"I want the full story of his killing. And you can start at the point where he gave you my money to, quote-unquote, invest."

"You're out of your fucking mind, Doyle," he growled. "If you think for a minute that I—"

I swung my right arm hard. The .22 in my hand caught BK flush in the face, sending his head snapping over the back of the chair. He yelped twice, a couple of high-pitched barks. A cut opened along his cheekbone, then blood flowed onto his nice linen shirt.

"The next one breaks a few teeth, Mr Whitney. Now, how much do you care for your son's well-being?"

"Doyle, you have no idea how dead you are!"

"Tell me what I want to know!"

"How about I tell you this? You and this street trash punk you brought with you can both go *fuck* yourselves!"

I took another swipe at BK's face. I heard cracking.

He howled again, then spit two teeth out, along with a good deal of his own blood.

"See what he thinks of you, BK?" I said softly. "Think he gives a shit what happens to you?"

I turned back to Whitney.

"The next one's gonna be even worse. You want to tell me about Sullivan's murder now?"

His right hand slid down off the desktop, obviously toward the top drawer. He was trying to be cool about it, but you could spot it a mile away.

"Hands on the desk!"

He put his hands back, palms down on the desk.

"Let's have it, Whitney. I'm running out of patience."

"You know what you can do," he replied.

I swung my arm up again, only this was the hand

that held the big nine millimeter. BK saw serious damage coming.

He shrieked, "No! No! I'll tell you! I'll tell you, Doyle!"

My arm stopped.

"Okay, let's have it."

"Will!" his father shouted. "Keep your mouth shut!"

BK hesitated, then looked back up at me. Through his bloody face, his eyes were desperate to talk. I knew he was going to tell it all.

Before he started, I reached past him into the breast pocket of the older Russian's sportcoat. I pulled out his handkerchief and gave it to BK.

"Here," I said. "Clean yourself up a little."

He wiped his mouth as well as his open face wound. The pain jabbed through him, I could tell. He was near tears.

"Goddammit!" Whitney roared. "Don't say anything!"

"Sure, don't say anything," BK moaned.

He tried to stop the blood draining from his big gashes. It flowed out anyway.

Tears finally made their way out. They were tears of physical pain, of course, but they were mixed with tears of emotional hurt, too. I knew those very well.

"You'd like that!" he cried. "I keep my mouth shut

while they beat the shit out of me, maybe kill me! You don't care about that, though, *do* you! Who the hell am I, anyway? I'm only your son. Your fucking son!"

He doubled over in agony. His sobbing was out of control.

After a minute, he got himself back together, sort of.

"All I wanted was to be mayor! That's all I ever fucking wanted. But you...you had to have...all this!" He spanned the room with his arm, including all the people in it.

Whitney's head dropped a little. He knew what was coming.

BK looked up at me through his tears.

He said, "It...it goes back before Sullivan invested the money. A couple of years ago, not long after I was elected...elected mayor, we did a sister-city exchange with this town—"

"I know about that," I interrupted.

"Well, what you probably didn't hear about was why we did it. It was so that the Russians could come and go from Key West without attracting any attention. Every time they showed up here, we just tied it to some made-up sister-city event."

Whitney leaped out of his chair.

"Will!" he bellowed. "Shut the fuck up!"

Shimmy raised his sawed-off to eye level, aiming it right at the old man.

"You shut the fuck up!" he cried. "And sit your fucking ass down! Or you won't have an ass to sit on!"

"Anyway," BK continued, "we got the sister-city thing set up because they want to be fully operational here when Cuba opens up."

He stopped and glanced around at the others in the room. The old man's gaze sliced through him. He knew, he absolutely knew, that things would never be the same.

Everything he'd wanted his whole life long, his name, his political career, everything, down the toilet.

The loser's look drew down over his bloody face.

"I know about the Cuba thing," I said. I pointed toward the older guy in the opposite chair. "Who's this?"

He continued putting pressure on his bleeding wound with the Russian's handkerchief. The blood kept coming.

"Mr Chernenko here is the organization's man in Moscow. His father was the Secretary General of the whole Soviet Union for about a year back around '84. Right before Gorbachev. He's using his political contacts to make sure the organization is welcome in Havana."

"When Castro goes."

"Right. Everything was coming together. It really was. Key West was going to be their American link to the new Cuba. Casinos, shipping, telephone service...shit, they're into all of that. And they want to control it all in Cuba."

I didn't tell him that Mambo had other plans.

Instead, I said, "So what's the connection between all that and Sullivan?"

"The Russians wanted his building for a strip joint."

"A strip joint?" I made like I didn't already know it.

"Well, yeah. Sullivan agreed to go along with it at first. He was going to be the quote, owner, unquote. But not the real owner, if you know what I mean."

He winced again at his pain as he brought the handkerchief back to his face.

"A front."

"That's right. He was well-liked around town and everybody knew him, so if he switched from Irish pub to strip club, people might think he'd lost a little common sense, but that'd be it. No one would really ask any serious questions."

"Like they might if a bunch of Russians suddenly and visibly took it over."

BK nodded. As he did, a steady flow of blood dripped all over his shirt and beyond, to the arm of

Whitney's expensive leather chair.

"Plus," he said, "Sullivan was leaning on us to help him get started with another Irish pub in Havana when the tourists started pouring in."

"And let me guess," I said. "The Russians didn't like that at all."

"Not at all."

He glared at Chernenko, then at Vasiliev.

Whitney almost jumped up from his chair again, but I quick-flicked my gun at him to settle him back down.

At that moment, I heard a few horns honking outside. It seemed like an intrusion into our private moment. They sounded like they were close to the house. I prayed nothing had happened to Doc, but the honking wouldn't stop.

BK said, "We just needed him to front the strip club, nothing more."

"What about the investment money?"

"We knew his lease was coming up for renewal this year. We did the investment thing two years ago to reel him in. Right about that time, the building came up for sale, so we bought it for good measure. To have something extra to hold over his head in case he got cold feet when the time came."

"And when the time came, he backed off and you

251

took his money."

"Well, hey, *I* didn't take it..."

"No," I said, glimpsing Whitney. "I know who took it. And I also know who's got it."

"Anyway," BK went on, "when Sullivan found out his money was gone, he went crazy. He said he wasn't going to let us take over his lease, that he was going to renew it as the Irish bar. I tried to talk some sense into him."

"You tried talking some sense into Sullivan?"

"I tried to tell him that he could make twice as much money with the Russians as he was making by himself, but he wasn't having any of it. Even my father here tried talking to him. He told my father if they tried any funny business, that he knew people in New Orleans that could take care of anyone who fucked with him. He said he wasn't afraid of us, or the Russians, or anybody."

I held back a little chuckle.

That was Sully, all right, and it got his ass killed.

I said, "And I came along right when you needed a patsy. It couldn't've been better timing."

"Like it was tailor-made. Ex-con just out of prison, comes back for his share of the dough, kills his partner over it, goes right back inside."

"That was the plan. Even when you were out here

to the house the first time."

Whoa, what was this?

"That was part of the setup?" I asked, not hiding my surprise.

"It was. My father got you out here just so he could tell you you'd never see your money unless Norma went back to the Fun House. Of course, he knew you wouldn't let her do that, and that you'd give him shit about it. He also knew you couldn't get the money, anyway. And Sullivan, by that time, was already a dead man, he just didn't know it. So when he was killed, you'd naturally think my father had it done to keep you from getting your money. You'd have no reason to think otherwise."

He soaked up more of his blood with the handkerchief. What the handkerchief missed went straight to the widening splotch on the chair.

"And so...everybody lives happily ever after," I said. "Everybody but Sully."

I looked over at Vasiliev.

"How about it, Yuri? You think you're gonna live happily ever after?"

The horns outside were now honking furiously. Everyone in the room was distracted by the long, loud bleats.

Amid the racket, BK lurched toward me.

"Don Roy!" he cried as he moved with his arms outstretched. "You've gotta believe me! I had nothing to do with Sullivan's death. These fucking Russians —"

Now that he was on his feet, he'd gotten between me and Vasiliev, right where I didn't want him, and Vasiliev took advantage of it.

He quickly reached under his shirt in his rear waistband as BK approached me. I caught the sudden move.

"BK!" I shouted. "Get down!"

I yanked at one of his hands, trying to jerk him to one side.

In one swift, catlike move, Vasiliev pulled a revolver and began firing. BK was hit from behind with the first shot and went down. The second caught me mid-thigh, pushing me back against the wall.

With BK out of the line of fire, I shot back several times, hitting Vasiliev in his side and his shoulder, spinning him around, then down to the floor. The revolver flew from his hand.

At the same moment, Alexei had drawn his spare piece, too, from an ankle rig, but Shimmy unleashed his twelve-gauge at Alexei's gut. It nearly tore him in half as he was sent hurtling backward into the wall. Some of Whitney's plaques cascaded to the floor.

A panicked Chernenko sprang out of his chair with

a gun he'd gotten from God knows where. I turned my two pistols on him, both blazing, sending him down.

Shimmy had zeroed in on Milton and Bradley. Milton froze in fear, terror all over his face, but Bradley dove toward the floor by the couch and retrieved one of the guns I'd kicked under there. Shimmy fired twice at his lunging figure, hitting him once in the ankle. Bone and blood spattered from his wound, staining the base of the couch's buttery leather.

From under the couch, he retrieved an automatic, pulling it up with both hands. He got off two quick rounds, one of them hitting Shimmy around the collarbone. The sawed-off fell to the floor as the shot flung him backward out of the office doorway.

I fired both of my automatics a bunch of times at Bradley, hitting him with almost every shot. He collapsed into a pool of his own blood, most of it flowing from two head wounds.

Sharp movement on my left grabbed the corner of my eye.

I wheeled around on one leg as best I could, seeing Vasiliev with blood pouring out of his side, crawling to where his spare piece had fallen.

He reached out for it.

"Don't try it, Yuri!"

He picked up the gun with an unsteady hand, then

rapidly raised it into firing position. I squeezed the trigger on the .22 and it just clicked.

Empty.

In an eyeblink, I did the same with the nine and caught him in the stomach with my last two shots. He fell backwards, his face stiffened by death.

My attention turned to the big desk. Whitney had reached inside his drawer and now held a revolver in his hand. With a firm grip, he took aim at me. I dropped to the floor the instant before he fired, landing on my wounded leg, nearly passing out from the sharp volts of pain.

From my prone position near the doorway to the office, I grabbed Shimmy's shotgun as Whitney aimed again. I had to get the shot off. Otherwise, I was a sitting duck.

This time, before I could shoot, a loud report came from the doorway behind me, just in time, right over my head. I saw Whitney stumbling back into his chair as a little red blotch appeared on his upper chest.

I looked up.

Ryder stood in the doorway, a smoking automatic in his hand.

"Where the hell were you?" I asked as I threw the shotgun aside.

I struggled to my feet.

"The plane arrived a couple of minutes early and they were gone by the time I got there."

Fucking government, I thought. Can't ever get it together.

Looking around, I could see BK groaning on the floor. He'd taken one in the shoulder blade, but it didn't look serious. Shimmy was still writhing in pain in the hallway, badly hit.

As I helped him up, I turned back to Milton, still paralyzed on the other side of the bloody office.

"You say whatever you want to the cops, Milton. Just leave me and Shimmy out of it. Got me?"

He nodded, still in shock.

"If the cops even *think* I was here tonight," I said, "you will have a very short life expectancy. I promise you that."

I looked back at Ryder.

"Get out of here," he said to me. "I'll take care of all this."

"Thanks," I said. "Safe's in the bedroom closet. It's open."

I grabbed the satchel. Shimmy and I limped out the door, bleeding and leaning on each other as best we could. I then saw what all the commotion outside was about.

Ryder had pulled his car into roadblock position in

the street, right behind where Doc sat in the parked Buick. The partygoers' cars were jammed up behind it, wall-to-wall honking horns and cursing drivers.

Even though I hurt like hell, I had to laugh.

Doc pulled the big deuce up directly in front of the house. We tumbled inside.

As he took off, he told us that with all the racket going on back there over Ryder's car, you couldn't really hear any of the shots from in the house. The ruckus was still going on as we sped off unnoticed into the night.

Shimmy was bleeding pretty badly. He let loose with a few tortured wails.

I told him, "Take it easy, bubba. We're gonna get us both fixed up right now."

Doc was full of concern, but still calm, as I knew he would be.

"Where to, man? We gotta get you taken care of."

"Turn right down here, then head back toward town. I know a guy who used to be a doctor."

SETUP ON FRONT STREET

THIRTY-THREE

The guy who fixed us up had one of Yale Lando's medical school degrees, which he'd gotten after they took his real one away. He pulled me and Shimmy through, all right, but we were hurting for many months afterward. Shimmy lost a little of the use of his left arm, but he's right-handed anyway, so there was no real harm done.

The doctor, meanwhile, may have plucked the bullet out of my thigh, but it was Norma who brought me back to health.

She looked after me in a way that I wasn't really expecting. You know, she really took care of me. She'd run and get me a drink of water if I was thirsty, she cooked all my meals for me, she waited on me hand and foot, that kind of thing. While I was recuperating, she showered me with love.

Let me tell you, nothing will bring you back faster

than that.

It meant everything to me, knowing that she really loved me that much.

I'd gotten a little over four hundred thousand of Whitney's money from his safe. Or should I say, *my* money. I gave Doc and Shimmy a hundred grand apiece, plus I paid for Shimmy's doctor bills, about another ten. That left me with right around two hundred large.

Which is what I had coming from the diamond deal in the first place.

I gave Doc an extra twenty-five hundred and told him when he got back to Vegas, to mail it to the guy whose Visa card I'd gotten from Yale. Charles Brockaway, that was his name. I figured Norma and I had gone through around fifteen hundred on our little spree up in Miami, so an extra grand worth of vig should take care of Brockaway.

I don't know, it just seemed like the right thing to do.

Ryder let Milton get away clean, then he split himself, right before the black-and-whites arrived.

First, though, he took the Russian papers in the safe.

Then he made sure to crack open the file cabinet and spread Whitney's files on Sullivan and Caribbean

Holdings all over the room. After checking through the files, the cops eventually found out that, after Sully's death, his wife hadn't renewed his lease on the bar, but that the owners, WA Properties, had leased it to Keys Good Times, Inc., with the stated intention of making it into a strip joint.

They also found what Ryder had showed me, that two Russians had applied for a liquor license to be used at that location. This alerted the FBI to possible mob activity, and Ryder later entered the picture "officially", making sure that Sully's connection to the whole thing was emphasized.

Gradually, then, the investigation of his murder shifted in that direction, toward the Russians, away from me, and Ortega was finally out of my face.

BK pulled through, and since he was the only known survivor of the bloodbath, he was heavily grilled by the cops. I'm told he put on a fine show for them.

His story, which I'm sure Ryder had helped him with that night before he left, was that BK and his father were discussing a legit real estate deal with the Russians, that he was naturally unaware of any of their criminal activities.

During this meeting, he said, a couple of armed Cubans came bursting in, shooting up the place, shouting "*¡Viva Cuba libre!*" Something about they knew there were Russians there and they were all pissed off over how the Russians and Castro ruined Cuba. For a couple of weeks afterward, everyone was on the lookout for gun-blasting Cubans.

The cops ate it up. So did the papers.

As soon as he recovered, though, BK resigned as mayor and left town. I don't know where he went.

Rita divorced him and stayed here. She continues to live in the big house on William Street. I see her around town from time to time.

I don't think she ever remarried.

As for me, I'm off the grift for good. I got me a straight job running Mambo's sports book and bolita game, generally taking care of things when he's not around.

Norma and I are back in her place and we've got this nest egg now. Sort of a little, I don't know...a little security...for the future.

This time I swear I'm not going to blow it, I'm not going near any dice tables anywhere, but I *am* going to take care of the woman I love, the most wonderful woman in the world.

Now, just in case you're wondering, I know the score here. I mean, I'm not stupid. I know there's an outside chance the Russians might eventually figure out what happened.

Most likely they won't, but if they do, they'll probably come looking for me.

And you know, I can't really blame them. They had big things cooking down here. They were set up pretty sweet, all ready to move into Cuba, until I derailed their whole deal.

So Norma and I had a long, long talk about it. We talked about moving, like to Miami or somewhere, or maybe leaving the state altogether.

But in the end, we just couldn't.

This is our home.

MIKE DENNIS

ABOUT THE AUTHOR

After thirty years as a professional musician (piano), Mike Dennis left Key West and moved to Las Vegas to become a professional poker player. In November 2010, his noir novel, *The Take*, was released by L&L Dreamspell. It's a story of human desperation set in Houston and New Orleans.

SETUP ON FRONT STREET

The Take is now available in both print and ebook on Amazon, Barnes & Noble online, Fictionwise, and All Romance.

In February, 2011, his collection of noir short stories, *Bloodstains On The Wall*, was released and is available digitally on Kindle, Barnes & Noble, and Smashwords. The print version is available on Amazon and CreateSpace.

In addition, Mike has had short stories published in A Twist Of Noir, Mysterical e, Slow Trains, and the 2009 Wizards Of Words Anthology.

Setup On Front Street is the first in a trio of Key West noir novels. The next one, *The Ghosts Of Havana*, will be coming soon.

In December 2010, Mike moved back to Key West.

http://mikedennisnoir.com